JEREMY THOMAS and FRANCIS BOUYGUES
present

A BERNARDO BERTOLUCCI FILM

LITTLE BUDDHA

LITTLE BUDDHA

**KEANU REEVES YING RUOCHENG CHRIS ISAAK
ALEX WIESENDANGER and BRIDGET FONDA**

Production and Costume Design JAMES ACHESON Editor PIETRO SCALIA

Cinematography VITTORIO STORARO AIC- A.S.C.

Music composed and conducted by RYUICHI SAKAMOTO

Story by BERNARDO BERTOLUCCI

Screenplay by RUDY WURLITZER and MARK PEPLOE

Producer JEREMY THOMAS Directed by BERNARDO BERTOLUCCI

LITTLE BUDDHA

A novel by Gordon McGill
Based on the screenplay by
Rudy Wurlitzer and Mark Peploe

BERKLEY BOOKS, NEW YORK

LITTLE BUDDHA

A Berkley Book / published by arrangement with
CiBy 2000, France

PRINTING HISTORY
Berkley edition / March 1994

ISBN: 0-425-14157-8

BERKLEY®
Berkley Books are published by The Berkley Publishing Group,
200 Madison Avenue, New York, New York 10016.
BERKLEY and the "B" design
are trademarks belonging to Berkley Publishing Corporation.

PRINTED IN THE UNITED STATES OF AMERICA

10 9 8 7 6 5 4 3 2 1

And he is born, he who will destroy the evil of rebirth. He will surrender sovereign power, he will master his passions, he will understand truth, and error will disappear in the world before the light of his knowledge.

—A. Ferdinand Herold,
The Life of Buddha

LITTLE BUDDHA

Prologue

In the monk's dream the old man smiled at him as he had smiled at death. While mourners held back their tears and prepared to weep, the dying man closed his eyes and chuckled at some private joke, and the monk heard him whisper, as if imparting a secret, that he had always found life amusing and saw no need to change now; and even as the soul of Lama Dorje moved on, the smile remained; even as the flesh stiffened; even as he passed through the transitional stage of *bardo*; even after the body had been burned on the funeral pyre, the rictus grin of the skull seemed to be mocking its condition.

In his dream the monk woke up and saw the old man alive again and beckoning him to follow him up a hill. The old man was dressed in blue trousers and the upper garment known in the West as a T-shirt, and a Western saying tried to nudge its way into the monk's mind—something about Rome. He snatched at it but it faded, and he concentrated on keeping up as the old man marched briskly toward the summit.

It was a suburban hill of clapboard houses set back behind sentry lines of sparse trees, the lawns trimmed as if by a beautician. The smell of pine mingled with rhododendron. It was a quiet, ordered place where children would be safe, even in this violent country.

The monk began to sweat and felt his calves stretch and ache, then mercifully the old man stopped and pointed to his right, at half an acre of fenced-off scrubland studded with the caterpillar tracks of earth-moving machines. A rectangular crater had been dug, and at first the monk thought that it must be some sort of mass grave, and he wondered at the strange mentality of the Westerners who buried their dead in boxes, but the old man was shaking his head at him, reading his mind, telling him by telepathy that this was the foundation of a house.

Beyond the far fence the ground dropped away steeply, and the monk could see the panorama of the city, with its tall glass buildings like dragons' teeth and the spindly, futuristic tower with its dish at the top and men and women moving about inside—tiny shapes, people living in the sky—and farther beyond, the sparkling blue of the bay and the mountains that reminded him of home.

He turned to ask the old man why they were here, but he had gone, and the monk began to worry that when he woke up, he would not remember or understand the significance. . . .

The monk blinked into the dawn. His calves were stiff, as if he had been climbing. Sweat trickled along the chubby contours of his body, and the dream coalesced into certainty, the images etched into his memory as if by acid. As he lay in his narrow bed in his austere little room, he felt honored that he had been chosen to be the messenger. The task would not be easy, but it had always been the Lama's way to set initiative tests for his brighter pupils, and the monk had no doubt that eventually he would find the crater in the ground at the top of the hill. There was no hurry. The child who was the old man would need time to grow before being put to the tests.

Part One

Part One

Part One

One

The bathroom mirror was mercifully misted by steam from the shower, and Dean Konrad shaved blind. By the time he had finished, it had cleared, and he glared at his reflection. He had the boiled-sweet eyes again, and his mouth was tacky from last night's whiskey. He reached for the eyedrops, squeezed them in, gargled mouthwash, then blinked at himself again.

"Thirty-five and still alive," he muttered. His eyes began to clear, and he smelt like a drugstore. He rubbed a thumb against his jaw. No sign of flab—yet. The other night Lisa had described him as looking "lived in" then had backtracked when he growled at her, saying it was a compliment. She used to call him "rugged." Now it was "lived in." Some fine semantic line had been crossed in the last few months. He had begun, for the first time, to look his age. Whiskey and worry were a bad combination. What he needed was a mouthwash for the brain.

As he toweled his hair dry, he tried to remember who had come up with the line that you don't drown your sorrows, you just teach them to swim. He couldn't remember. Some smart-ass who didn't have a new mortgage that was about to transform itself into a repossession order.

A blast of caffeine and he was ready for the drive to the airport. He dressed in the bedroom and strapped on his watch. Five-thirty, which meant four hours' sleep, and even four hours were getting to be a luxury; but there was no choice, not with the wolves at the door. He picked up his bag and looked down at Lisa, prettily, blondly asleep, Lisa of the perfect cheekbones. He kissed her throat. She grabbed his thumb and came blearily awake, but he shushed her and whispered that it was too early, and as he went out, he heard her mumble bye-bye and not to forget to phone from the airport.

He padded along the corridor and into Jesse's room. A shaft of moonlight lit the boy up. He was lying on his back, arms stiffly by his sides, sleeping at horizontal attention and grinning like a rogue. Dean smiled. Children were supposed to look like cherubs when they were asleep, all innocent and lovable. Not Jesse. He looked as if he were planning mayhem.

The dawn was breaking as Dean went outside,

and for the first time since spring he could see his breath. As he backed the car out onto the hill, he looked out at the million-dollar view of the city and the bay and the mountains. It was a magnificent panorama. At least he could still admire it. He had not become blasé. He still had his sense of wonder.

So far . . .

For Lisa, it was turning out to be a normal day: a wake-up call from Dean just before he boarded; an inquisition from Jesse over breakfast, which already she couldn't remember; then school. Third grade had been boisterous. Some of the older boys had been slyly lecherous. Grade Five, the problem class, had been sullen and unresponsive. When she looked into those dull faces, there were times that she wished she had taken up history so that she could tell stories to the children rather than attempt to interest them in the wonders of pi. But then there were the bonuses: the little girl with the curls, the ten-year-old tough kid with the big brain, both naturals, both inevitably bound for college, the only two interested in the subject for its own sake, the only two who saw beauty in geometry.

And Jesse. As she eased the little Volkswagen off the freeway, Lisa wondered which direction he would take. Right now he was an all-rounder with no specific leaning toward any one subject, but there was time. What he had was the blessed combination of limitless curiosity and boundless opportunity. She went through a count-your-blessings chant, like a mantra, thanking God or whomever or whatever for Dean and Jesse and a beautiful home in a pristine, drug-free, virtually crime-free zone. As she got out of the car and sucked in a lungful of early autumn air, she told herself for the umpteenth time that if she couldn't bring up an eight year old to become a well-adjusted, well-educated young man with the world at his feet in Seattle, Washington, the last bastion of liberalism—then, Lisa, you gotta be some kind of failure.

She walked across to the school fence and watched the children playing, looking out for the Seahawks jacket and the blond head, and she was so intent on searching for him that she did not notice that she was being studied, not until the voice behind her made her jump.

"A beautiful day."

She turned to see a small, bald, chubby man dressed in maroon robes. His arms were folded inside the wide sleeves, and he was smiling at her. Maybe sixty, she thought, and wrinkle-free, like a grown-up baby. She agreed about the weather and turned back to the fence.

"I'm a Buddhist monk."

Ah, she thought. Good. Fine.

"From Tibet."

The voice was hard to place, no obvious accent, no lilt to get a fix on, no fodder for instant judgment or prejudice.

"My name is Kempo Tenzin."

She turned again and looked down at him. He

bowed. His smile broadened, the little eyes vanishing between folds of fat.

"I am teaching here," he said.

She tried to make her "Oh, really?" sound genuine.

He bowed again, and she had an urge to take him home, give him a fishing rod, build him a pond, and surround him with plaster gnomes. He seemed to be waiting for a reaction.

"I'm a teacher too," she said.

He nodded.

"Math."

This news pleased him. "Like me," he said. "Also I teach astrology. Mostly astrology."

"That's unusual," she said weakly, waiting for the inevitable follow-up. What was her star sign? But it didn't come.

"Tibetans have a very advanced system of astrology," he said.

But she was no longer listening. She had spotted Jesse and waved at him. The monk moved closer, and she was aware of a strange smell, like slightly off butter, mixed with incense. She looked at him again. Now he not only looked like a baby, but he smelled like one—baby-milk and dope—a sort of fat, old, baby hippie, and she had to stifle a smile.

He looked across the yard as Jesse ran toward them, then he said, "May I ask on which day your son was born?"

Her first reaction was to snap a what's-it-to-you? at him, but the face was so innocent and the voice so inoffensively inquisitive that she told him: March first.

"And at what hour?"

"In the morning. Early. At six-thirty I think."

The reaction was extraordinary. He clapped his hands and danced a little jig. It was as if he had won the state lottery.

"Wonderful, wonderful," he said. "Six-thirty. Very special."

She was about to ask what was so special about giving birth at dawn in March, but Jesse had launched himself at the fence and was making silly monkey faces at her, and she was only vaguely aware of the monk handing her a business card. Then he was backing away, and she was briefly reminded of something she had once read: You don't turn your back on royalty. But Jesse had started his first inquisition of the afternoon, and she forgot all about Kempo Tenzin. . . .

He watched them go—the tall, slim beauty in the suit, the little boy bounding along next to her. Then mother and son hugged at the gate, and Kempo Tenzin hugged himself in delight. He had passed the test. Now all he had to do was find a post office and a machine that would send the news back home.

Two

On the September morning that came to be known as the Day of the Telegram, the young monk named Chompa was daydreaming. He sat at a window beneath the eaves of the ancient monastery and gazed north at the mountains and the unmarked border of Bhutan and Tibet.

He was thinking of his parents and the two-day trek he had made five years earlier to the pass, carrying their ashes in a brass urn hidden in his robes. They had died within a week of each other, and he had fulfilled his promise to scatter their ashes in the country they had fled twelve years before he was born. Their only fear, as they made him promise, was that he might be caught by the soldiers, but he had evaded them easily, both going there and coming back. Not even the Chinese with their multitudes could patrol the Himalayas.

He remembered that Tibet had looked much like Bhutan, yet from that day he had felt a longing to go back, to see Lhasa perhaps and certainly to die in his parents' country. Surely by then the Chinese would have gone. Surely in forty or fifty years, when his time came, the Chinese would have come to their senses. . . .

"Now then. Pay attention. . . ."

The Lama's voice punctured his reverie, and he turned away from the window.

The old man was about to tell another of his stories. He sat on a dais next to a life-size stone effigy of the Buddha, and, not for the first time, Chompa thought how alike they were: the same bulk, the same bull-like neck and shoulders, the same benign expression. If the Buddha's eyes could twinkle, they could have been brothers.

The twenty boy monks, arranged in a semicircle in front of the old man, needed no telling to pay attention. Lama Norbu was famous for his stories. His voice was deep, his gaze hypnotic, and Chompa, scanning the boys in their maroon robes, their heads shaved to black stubble, was reminded of cobras before a mongoose.

The Lama began his story, speaking in a whisper so that the boys had to concentrate.

"It was in the ancient days," he said, "long before even this place was built and out there"—he pointed at the window, and twenty heads swiveled—"a crowd of villagers stood in front of a stone altar."

Chompa had heard the story often enough, of the goat about to be sacrificed in order to ensure a good harvest, and just as the knife was drawn, it had spoken to the High Priest, laughing in his face and telling him how pleased he was to die again.

The old man told the story from both points of view, imitating the priest's voice, mimicking the goat's bleat.

"'After four hundred and ninety-nine times dying,' the goat said, 'and being reborn as a goat, I will be reborn as a human being.'"

One of the younger boys clapped. Chompa shushed him, and the boy's face went as red as his robes.

The Lama continued: "The goat said, 'I am thinking of you, poor priest. Five hundred lives ago I too was a priest, and like you, I sacrificed goats to the gods.' At that, the priest dropped to his knees and said, 'Forgive me, I beg you. From now on I will be the guardian and protector of every goat in the land.'"

The youngest boy's mouth dropped open, and Chompa stared at him, sending a mental message: *Open your mouth and catch mosquitoes.* The boy's mouth snapped shut.

Quietly the old man continued, telling how the goat knew that his time had come, and, sure enough, from a mountain peak a thunderbolt zipped down the slope, bounced off rocks, and struck it dead.

"Its head spun through the air," the Lama said, "and landed in front of the kneeling priest. It was smiling."

Silence now, the room a frozen tableau.

"Now then," the old man said. "What does this ancient tale tell us?"

In chorus, they shouted: "That no living creature must ever be sacrificed."

Lama Norbu raised the index finger of his right hand. "For he who commits an evil deed . . ."

"Will surely suffer an evil result," they replied.

Lama Norbu nodded and smiled, satisfied with their responses.

The smallest monk still looked worried. He raised a tiny hand, and Lama Norbu acknowledged him.

"What happened to the goat?"

"Ah yes, the goat. The goat had many lives as a human being, until one day he turned into someone very strange indeed. . . ." The Lama paused dramatically, then suddenly pointed. "He became—Chompa."

Chompa took his cue, dropped to his hands and knees, and cavorted around the room, bleating and shaking his head. He made a good goat. The boys cheered and clapped their appreciation, and Lama Norbu and the Buddha beamed at them. Then the noise died down as the door opened, and an old man came in. He was holding an envelope. He bowed to Lama Norbu and handed it over.

The Lama looked puzzled. It was the first time a telegram had been delivered to the monastery.

The outside world, the world of sea-level, was beginning to encroach. He put on his spectacles, read carefully, and beamed at Chompa.

"I have been waiting for eight years to receive this," he said, and Chompa was about to ask what it was when a gong sounded and the boy monks, as one, looked at the old man like hungry chicks.

"I can see by your empty expressions," he said, "that your stomachs are now fully in control of your minds, so you had better go and fill them."

They needed no further bidding, and within seconds the two men were alone.

"Is it about Lama Dorje?" Chompa asked.

Lama Norbu nodded.

"Have they found him?"

"Perhaps."

"Perhaps" was enough for Chompa. "Perhaps" meant the possibility of seeing the world. If "perhaps" could become a probability, then he, as the old man's favorite pupil, would go on the search. He would leave the mountains and go down to the earth below and into an airplane and over the oceans. The very idea made him feel dizzy.

The old man had a bad night of cold perspiration and nightmares. The face of Mara, the Lord of Darkness, mocked him, and in his sleep he feared death and Mara laughed at his weakness. In his waking hours, he had no fear of the death that was imminent, no fear that this particular life was coming to an end, but in his sleep, Mara stripped away the protective armor of his faith and terrorized him as if he were no more than a nonbeliever.

He wakened slowly and swung himself off the cot. His back ached, but he ignored it. On an altar beneath the window stood two butter lamps. He lit them, and the room glowed dully yellow. It was as small as a cell, just the bed and the wooden altar cluttered with bowls and a framed photograph of an old man grinning at the camera and pulling his left earlobe.

Lama Norbu sat before the altar and bowed his head in meditation. Within seconds he began to lose track of time. An hour passed. Then another. The light began to change, the first paleness of dawn seeping through the slats of the shutters. A cock crowed. The old man opened his eyes, then got painfully to his feet, stepped back, and prostrated himself before the altar, touching his forehead to the floor three times and mumbling a mantra. Perspiration oozed in tiny droplets on his forehead and upper lip. His breathing rasped. He got up and opened the shutters. Pale pinkness glistened on the Himalayan peaks. He had never grown tired of the view. To weary of such a sight was to mock the soul.

He picked up the frame and peeled the photograph out, touched it to his forehead, and placed it in the trunk, then began packing: two maroon robes, a collection of woolen undergarments, an armful of loose-leaf books of scripture. Then he sat again on the bed and took a deep breath. The sound was unhealthy, a rasp like wood being sawn. He took a small box from the altar, opened it, and placed a black pill beneath his tongue. The pills would prolong this particular life, at least until his job was done. He would not deign to ask the Buddha for favors, but he hoped that his wish would be granted, to meet Lama Dorje again before he died.

An hour later he walked out into the morning air and slowly made his way down the outside staircase toward the courtyard. Behind him, two young monks carried the trunk with two suitcases lying on top. Behind them, Chompa walked slowly, trying to look solemn, not wanting his excitement to seem obvious.

They crossed the courtyard and walked along a portico. At the end, two old monks were working on a mandala spread on a trestle table. It was a circle of sand, six feet in diameter, and they were marking out an intricate diagram. Briefly Lama Norbu stopped, looked at it, then continued, only to stop again as an ancient man appeared in a doorway, tall, lame, and oozing dignity. He was supported by a young monk.

The Lama went up to him and presented his *kata*. The old man blessed the white scarf and, as tradition demanded, placed it on the Lama's right shoulder.

"We shall all pray for the success of your mission," he said in a wheezing voice.

"Thank you, Abbot," the Lama said. They touched foreheads, then the procession made its way toward the main gate.

"And remember to take your medicine," the Abbot shouted after them.

The Lama nodded and went down a flagstoned path to a covered bridge that spanned the river. Halfway across, their way was blocked by a wild man. He wore filthy furs. A yellow bone protruded from his matted, shoulder-length hair. His ears were pierced with jade, and a crooked grin creased his weathered face.

He held up one hand to stop them, then with the other produced a wooden bowl from the recesses of the furs and held it out. At first Chompa thought the wild man was begging, but then he bowed and cleared his throat, and when he spoke, his voice crackled from lack of use.

"This bowl belonged to Lama Dorje," he said. "He gave it to me before I left thirteen years ago to live in my cave. You will need it for your search."

Chompa stared at him, trying to remember. He must have been about ten when he last saw this man. Then he had been straight, bright-eyed, and well-muscled, but he had chosen the way of the ascetic to find salvation. He had probably never spoken in all these years, and Chompa wondered if it hurt. He was laughing at some private joke now as he cleaned the bowl on his elbow.

"Lama Dorje always insisted that everything be clean," he said. "Including me."

Chompa frowned, thinking that he was being irreverent toward the Lama, but the old man showed no sign of irritation. Instead, he bowed as he accepted the bowl.

"And how is your retreat going?" he asked.

"As I expected. When I entered the cave, I was a

complete fool. Now that I have come out for a day, I realize that I am an even bigger fool."

This struck him as hilarious. He shook his head, uttered a shriek of laughter, then turned, ran back across the river, and vanished into the woods.

Again the old man slowly set off, and Chompa followed him across the bridge, then turned and looked south, toward the place called sea level, where they would get into an airplane and fly across the ocean into the future known as America.

Three

The young Customs officer was coming to the end of his shift and, as usual these days, running out of tolerance. Lately he had come to realize that the job was corrupting him. He had started out as an open-minded liberal with all the proper, politically correct responses, but after two years he was becoming a bit of a bigot. No longer did he automatically hold out the hand of welcome to the poor and the huddled masses; two years of discovering contraband in their luggage and slyness in their affectations of innocence had coarsened him, and he had wondered, if he, Steve McGovern, a nice college boy from a family of Democrats in the northwest, could fall prey to prejudice, what chance had his colleagues in New York or Miami or the Rio Grande Border Patrol? He was becoming jaundiced. Last time out he had voted for Bush.

He checked his clipboard. The next batch due in was an Air India from New Delhi. Another consignment of sarongs, saris, and sandals. Maybe he'd get lucky. Maybe Joe and Big Mick down there in Immigration would get bilious, allow only Americans in, and send the rest back to the Pacific Rim. Then he looked up, and the face that once instinctively smiled at strangers set into a scowl.

He glanced at Harry at the next desk then focused on the first two coming toward them. Maroon robes and shaved heads. The big one was an older version of George Foreman, the young one moonfaced and gazing around him in wonder. They were like some sort of vaudeville team, and they were heading for the green channel with their two little bags and a trunk on a trolley, a trunk that looked like it came out of the Ark.

No, you don't, guys.

"Excuse me, gentlemen." McGovern's words were curdled with sarcasm, the second finger of his left hand twitching, ordering them over. The young one steered the trolley toward him. He looked at it and saw that it was made of wood with all sorts of intricate carvings, and he wondered what kind of an excess they had had to pay to bring this baby in.

The young one opened it. Hinges creaked. The old one watched closely as McGovern went through the contents. There was a musty smell of sour butter and incense, and McGovern's nostrils twitched. He looked up at the old man, and the first word that flashed to mind was a cliché: *inscrutable*.

Wrong, he thought; more than that. He searched for the word, thinking back to his English classes. *Avuncular*, maybe. No. The old guy was looking at him like he felt sorry for him. *Compassionate*. That was it, and McGovern's irritation festered into annoyance.

"Are you carrying any drugs or firearms, any fruits or vegetables?" The question was put in a monotone, rat-a-tat, like a cop reading a suspect his rights.

"No," the old man said.

Roughly McGovern groped among robes and underclothing, dragging the clothes out, and gazed into an Aladdin's cave of old bowls, trinkets, drums, and little, potbellied, grinning Buddhas until he saw what he was looking for—something to wipe the smug compassion off the old boy's face. The dagger had a vicious, triangular blade. He held it up and whistled. Stick that in flesh and the wound would never heal. He squinted at the hilt, fashioned in the shape of some hideous griffin.

"What's this for?" he said aggressively.

"It is a religious object," the old man explained. "It is used to cut through the bonds of ignorance."

Sure, McGovern thought; cut through a jugular easy.

"Well," he said. "It looks like a weapon to me."

Strike one, he thought and laid the dagger on

25

the table. As he resumed his search, he heard a familiar voice behind him say, "It's okay." McGovern turned to see his boss coming across the room—Roger who could spot a smuggler at a hundred yards, Roger of the X-ray eyes and suspicious mind, a man so often right that he had a reputation for being telepathic, and now he did an extraordinary thing. He stood in front of the old man, placed his palms together, and bowed, then he picked up the knife and put it back in the trunk.

"You may proceed, Lama," Roger said. "And welcome to Seattle."

Lama?

McGovern blinked as he watched the two men in maroon robes wander off to the exit, and then he remembered. A lama was a priest, wasn't it? So the rumors were true. Roger was a goddamn Buddhist after all. Maybe that was where he got his telepathy from.

Amen, McGovern said to himself; two more crazies with a knife in the land of the free; a drop in the ocean.

Chompa's first impression as he scanned the crowds in the Arrivals Hall was of bewildering variety: so many different complexions and hair colors, so many different types of clothes and hats, and almost everyone with some kind of message. People passed him by announcing that they were Coca Cola or a Seahawk or a New York Met, a Superbowl or a Hollywood. The hats all bore letters, the shirts had numbers on their backs—it was mystifying. And such tight clothing on both men and women, so uncomfortable, and so much exposed flesh that he had to close his eyes for a moment to damp down the flickering fire of *samsara*. Then, when he looked again, he saw a reassuring slash of maroon through the glass wall that led to America and recognized Kempo Tenzin waving at him—fat little Tenzin, whom Chompa had not seen since he was a boy.

Lama Norbu was already moving toward him, and Chompa had to move fast to catch up, pushing his trolley up to the Lama's side and past him so that he would be the first to step into America. Then he blinked, startled as the glass wall hissed and parted without a hand touching it, and Tenzin was through, bowing and saying welcome and pointing to something called a parking lot.

Chompa's brain could not take in the sights through the windows. He grew uncomfortably aware of Lama Norbu's disapproval and realized that his mouth was open and his tongue limp on his bottom lip. *Open your mouth and catch mosquitoes.* He clamped it shut so fast that he bit his tongue.

The freeways, as Tenzin called them, swooped over bridges and across water, joining up and separating again like so many ant trails, but with cars speeding along them. And the buildings were surely a mirage, some kind of optical illusion, like a mandala only without any symmetry.

Lama Norbu had tried to prepare him, telling him about the phenomenon known as jet lag and warning of something called culture shock, but he could not cope with this place called Seattle and listen to Tenzin at the same time; and so he closed his eyes.

". . . they began about a month after he died," Tenzin was saying. "Always the same."

Lama Norbu listened intently as the monk described the dream, interrupting only once.

"Jeans?" he said. "He was wearing jeans?"

"Oh, yes," Tenzin said, chuckling. "When in Rome, do as the Romans do. It's a Western saying."

Then he chattered on excitedly, telling how he had turned detective, how he had taken his bearings from the building called the Space Needle.

"See," he said pointing to the tower that dominated the skyline. "Beautiful, isn't it? One of the highest buildings on the West Coast. Six hundred and five feet tall. And the bay, see. It's called Puget Sound, and the hill over there is Mount Rainier."

Chompa opened his eyes, thinking that perhaps Tenzin was guilty of the sin of pride in his adopted country, but it did not matter. If it were a sin, it was a very minor one. The voice chattered on excitedly.

"I went to the site often, whenever the dream returned, but it was always empty until last year, when one day I saw they had started to build a house."

The words tumbled out of him: how he watched the house being built, then saw the family move in, how the woman with her yellow hair was so beautiful, and the little boy so handsome with the

28

same fine yellow hair, how he found out that their name was Konrad.

"How?" Lama Norbu interrupted.

"On their mailbox," Tenzin said.

How he could not bring himself to approach them or ring their doorbell, and Chompa sleepily nodded agreement. Respect for privacy was paramount.

Tenzin told how he had seen Jesse at the local school and how one day he had taken a deep breath and just walked up to the boy's mother at the fence. . . .

And Chompa fell asleep.

Lisa was at her desk correcting algebra papers when she heard the doorbell ring. Immediately she heard Maria moving in the kitchen, and she yelled, "Okay, I'll get it," then yawned her way downstairs, thinking it was probably Sally from next door and it would be good to get some coffee brewing and take a break. And as she reached the door, she thought for the hundredth time how nice it was to live in a place where you don't need peepholes and chains and . . . She opened the door and saw the little old baby in his maroon robes.

He gave a deep bow, straightened, and said, "Mrs. Konrad. Do you remember me?"

How could she forget, but what was his name again, and what was he doing following her, and how had he found the house? She just said yes and waited. Then she remembered the business card.

"Ah, yes, your card with the invitation to your"—she had forgotten the word, then it came to her—"Dharma Center. I'm afraid I just haven't had the time."

He shrugged and glanced back, and she saw another one of them at the gate, a big, bull-like man, watching them, and for a moment she felt apprehensive and glad that Maria was in the house, just in case.

"I hope we are not disturbing you," Tenzin said.

He was, but it didn't matter; he was just disturbing algebra. Besides, he was so damn sweet and unintrusive, not like the Jehovah's Witnesses or the scary Moonies or the Mormons with their feet in the door.

"You see, my friend Lama Norbu"—he nodded in the big man's direction—"has just arrived from Bhutan."

Bhutan? Think. Himalayas, right?

"He is a very important lama." He paused while Lisa struggled for something to say that would not sound banal.

"He has never been in America before."

Tenzin shuffled in his sandals, looking embarrassed.

"And I was wondering . . ." he said.

"Yes?"

"I was wondering . . . if it would be possible . . . he has come on a very special mission."

Lisa smiled and put him out of his misery by asking them in. Again the beam. Again he had won the state lottery. "Yes, yes," he said, beckoning the old man over. "It will be very interesting for him." As the Lama came up to her and Tenzin made the introductions, she thought: Buddhists are pacifists, right? Literally wouldn't harm a fly. The opposite of crazies. I can let these people into my house, can't I? Sure.

She led them up the stairs, apologizing for the mess.

"We only just moved in a few weeks ago. My husband designed the house. He's an architect."

She showed them into the living room with its curved wall of glass and the million-dollar view of the city, the bay, and the mountains. Two chairs, a sofa, a coffee table, and still undecorated, still, as she had joked with Dean, "unlived in." Unlike his face.

She watched the Lama walk straight to the coffee table and pick up the framed photo, the one taken at the ski lodge with her smiling up at Dean, with Jesse between them tugging at his ear. He gazed intently at it, and she noticed that it was Jesse he was studying.

"As you can see," she said, "we're still living out of crates."

Lama Norbu put the picture down. "Very beautiful," he said. "Very empty."

Lisa chuckled at the description. "Yes," she said. "My husband loves emptiness. He wants to keep it this way." Moving right along now, she thought, what do you offer Tibetans?

Coffee?

No.

Tea?

No thanks.

And no social banter. They just sat down, Tenzin on a chair, the Lama on the floor, cross-legged. Then he took his shoes off.

A movement at the door made her turn. Maria was standing in the doorway, gazing at the men.

"Missus Konrad," she said, not taking her eyes off them. "Is it all right if I leave now?"

"Yes. Fine. See you tomorrow."

But she did not move, and Lisa knew what she was thinking. Maria was in a protective mode now, unwilling to leave her alone with these peculiar people.

"It's okay, Maria," she said. "Off you go."

She went reluctantly, Lisa shooing her like a dog. Then Lisa turned back and smiled, waiting for whatever they wanted of her.

"Lama Norbu is also a teacher," Tenzin said. "He was my teacher. In our monastery in Bhutan."

"I see." A roomful of teachers; a quorum even.

"He has come on a very important mission for all of us. He will stay at the Dharma Center we started in Oakville."

Lisa heard herself say, "I see," again, then she asked the Lama if this was his first time in America.

"Oh, yes. The first time."

She waited. They seemed reluctant to come to the point. They were polite to the point of absurdity. A silence. She was becoming impatient and was relieved to hear the front door open.

"That must be Dean," she said, and excused herself.

He was trudging up the stairs. Not long ago he used to run up the stairs and cavort around the place, six-one, a hundred and eighty pound package of vitality. Now he trudged.

"You look done in," she said as they kissed.

"I am."

Just that. No explanation. She wasn't going to ask "What's wrong?" again and get a curt "Nothing." He'd tell her in due course.

"Come on," she said, pushing him toward the living room door. "I've a little distraction for you,"

He looked in, saw the men, and took a step backward.

"Who are these guys?"

She suppressed a giggle. He sounded just like Newman doing Butch Cassidy, and she was going to do a Redford, saying, "Just keep thinkin', Butch, that's what you're good at," but there wasn't time.

"I don't know," she said. "They just appeared."

He glanced into the room again.

"The round one is a teacher of astrology," she said.

"And the square one?"

"The teacher's teacher."

"And where's Jesse?"

"Doing his homework."

She led him in. The Tibetans stood and bowed as Lisa made the introductions.

"I met Mr. Tenzin a few weeks ago, darling," Lisa said. "At Jesse's school."

"Ah. Yeah." He'd forgotten. She had told him that night when he phoned from San Francisco. It hadn't registered. The news that some monk had turned up asking when Jesse was born hadn't seemed front page material at the time.

Another hiatus as the Tibetans sat again. Dean looked at the Lama on the floor, then at his shoes gaping up at him like empty mouths from the floor.

"Our friends were admiring the emptiness of the room," Lisa said.

"Right," Dean said. "Nothing can be empty enough for me."

"Emptiness is a big subject," Lama Norbu said to Lisa, then turned to Dean. "Like zero for a mathematician. But no room will be empty if the mind is full." He smiled at Tenzin. "You learn that in a prison cell."

Lisa shot a glance at Dean and guessed what he was thinking. He was thinking: Christ, these guys are ex-cons. In my house.

And how about the dialogue. Like something out of a fortune cookie. And it looked like there was more to come. The Lama looked at Dean again.

"All form is about emptiness," he said.

Then to Lisa.

"Every cause has its effect."

Then to them both, switching from one face to the other as he spoke.

"Everything is impermanent, and nothing happens by chance. One should be nonviolent to oneself, to others, to nature. Buddhists believe these things."

Well, Lisa thought, it's all or nothing with you,

friend. No small talk here; it's either silence or profundity. Then the Lama laughed.

"But I see I teach too much," he said.

Dean rubbed his eyes. "Honey," he whispered, "I need a scotch."

"So do I," she whispered back, trying not to be rude, but the two men seemed deep in thought, as if meditating. She started to get up but the Lama suddenly leaned forward and gazed at them.

"Now I must explain our mission."

Dean pulled her back down beside him. The scotch would have to wait.

"We come from Tibet. For many years we have been in exile, the guests of our brothers in Bhutan, Nepal, and India."

"Since the occupation," Tenzin said. "Nineteen fifty-nine."

Dean nodded, and Lisa sighed with relief. So that was what he meant by the prison cell. The Chinese invasion of Tibet. It had happened not long before she was born. The Dalai Lama fleeing across the mountains. Terrible stories of atrocities by the Chinese troops. . . .

"It is the practice of Buddhism that keeps the spirit of the Tibetan people alive," the Lama continued. "In Tibetan Buddhism we believe that everybody is reborn again and again, but there are a very few beings who, by reaching Enlightenment, could escape from this endless circle of deaths and rebirths and attain Nirvana. But they decide voluntarily, after death, to come back to help others. We believe these very special beings come back as spiritual guides, particular people whom we can identify." He paused. "That is why we are here."

"You mean," Dean said, "you're here to find someone."

Lisa heard the sarcasm in his voice, the tired, disbelieving drawl, and she hoped that the Tibetans hadn't picked up on it, because there was something about the old man's voice, so deep, melodious, hypnotic that a sacrilegious thought sneaked into her mind. It was the voice of a seducer.

"Yes," he said. "My old teacher, Lama Dorje. We are looking for his reincarnation."

Dean exhaled sharply, and Lisa searched for something to say, something more than just an "Oh really," but the Lama was looking at the door now. She turned and saw a red, whiskered nose poke into the room, three feet off the ground.

"Jesse," Lisa said, "come and say hello."

The boy in his papier-mâché mask came slowly into the room and gazed at the Tibetans, then pulled on his left earlobe, and Lisa knew he was concentrating. It was a habit he had had from birth. He was in stockinged feet. Slowly he crossed the room and poked his right foot into the Lama's shoe.

"This is Lama Norbu, darling," Lisa said. "And you've already met Kempo Tenzin."

Jesse raised his mask, and his hair flopped over his forehead, fine, silken blond strands that Sally had said could sell shampoo.

"Why don't you wear your shoes?" he said.

Not hello or how are you. Just straight to the point, like his father.

The Lama smiled. "It's an old Tibetan habit." He pointed at Jesse's feet. Jesse nodded, taking the point, then pulled on his mask again and asked the Lama in a muffled voice if he liked it.

"In my country we love masks."

"I made it. It's a red rat." Then he turned and ran out, and they heard him clattering down the stairs.

"I will explain," the Lama said. "I was the pupil of a very great Lama, a truly holy man. Lama Dorje was even a teacher of the Dalai Lama, our great spiritual leader. Toward the end of his life Lama Dorje believed it was important to spread the Dharma to the West, so he came to the United States, where he passed away eight years ago. We have been searching for his reincarnation in many places. And now we think he might have been reborn right here, as your son."

Lisa wheezed out, "Jesse?" Then she was literally, temporarily struck dumb. She was conscious of her jaw dropping. Normally whenever anyone said anything stupid, her sense of flippancy rose like a fish to a fly. Normally she would have immediately come out with something witty, some put-down line, but not now. It was as if her brain had been sprayed with Mace.

Then Kempo Tenzin burst into a fit of giggling. "Lama Dorje had a great sense of humor."

She looked at Dean. He hadn't seen the joke. He held up both hands in front of his face like a boxer waiting for the next jab; then he leaned forward and spoke slowly, enunciating each syllable as if he could not trust the words to come out in the right order.

"Let me understand this clearly. You think that our son, Jesse, could be the actual reincarnation of your Tibetan teacher?"

That's my boy, Lisa thought; quick on the up-take as usual.

"Yes," the Lama said, smiling. "Please don't be angry."

Dean shook his head, then began to laugh. "That's amazing," he said. "It's the most unbelievable thing I ever heard."

The Tibetans nodded in agreement.

"Of course, we are not sure yet," the Lama said. "It is very difficult to know. Almost as difficult as it is to believe."

Lisa glanced at Dean, wondering what he would do next—probably throw them out and reach for the whiskey bottle. Then they heard the sounds of footsteps on the stairs, and Jesse came in with yet another surprise, a young monk with a pleasant, round face, eyes puffy as if he had just woken up.

"This is Chompa," Jesse said proudly, as if he owned him.

Chompa bowed. He was carrying three packages, two wrapped in muslin, the other in paper.

"Ah," said the Lama. "You have woken up." He turned to Dean and Lisa. "Please excuse us," he said. "Chompa was very tired and fell asleep in the car. We arrived this afternoon from Bhutan. It was a very long flight."

Again Dean and Lisa gazed astonished at each other; then Dean spoke slowly, as if to a backward child.

"You arrived today? From Bhutan? And you came straight here?"

The three men nodded. Chompa handed the muslin packages to the Lama, who handed one to Lisa and the other to Dean.

Jesse frowned.

"Why are they giving you presents, Mom?" he asked, and Lisa caught the inflection, the emphasis on the word *you*. Like, why am I not getting anything? Nonetheless, it was a good question. Why give presents to strangers?

Again she caught a whiff of rancid butter mixed with incense as she unwrapped the muslin and picked out a small bronze bell, intricately carved. Dean unwrapped a small bronze scepter.

"The bell represents Silence," the Lama said. "The scepter represents Compassion."

"Beautiful," Dean said. "Just what I need."

There it was again, the curdled sarcasm. Lisa glanced at the old man, but if he had noticed the insult, he did not show it. Instead, he bowed once more.

"It was a great honor to meet you," he said. "Now we must leave."

Jesse twitched with impatience and tugged his sleeve. "Are we going to see you again?" he said.

"I hope so. Certainly."

"You should see the monorail," Jesse said, flushed with excitement now. He turned to Dean.

"Shouldn't they, Dad? I'll show them the monorail."

"It's very kind of you," the Lama said, "but I think it's up to your parents."

"I haven't got school tomorrow, Mom." Jesse was pleading now, and Lisa felt trapped, painted into a corner.

"Well," she said, "I suppose Maria could go . . ."

Then Dean made the decision. "Sure," he said, "you can show them around."

Jesse whooped with delight. Then the Lama bent toward him, took the third package from Chompa, handed it to him, and touched his forehead gently against Jesse's.

"And this is for you . . . and tomorrow you will be my guide."

"Yeah."

Guide? thought Lisa. His old teacher was his guide. This was getting curiouser and curiouser.

And then they were gone, and only a whiff of butter and incense remained.

A million-dollar view; that was what the realtor had said when he was trying to sell him the land. Dean looked out and sipped whiskey. The man had not exaggerated. The evening sky was streaked pink. The mountains glistened with autumn snow. The city twinkled like terrestrial starlight, the dish of the Space Needle glowing yellow. Not so long ago he had felt almost godlike up here, gazing down upon transparent anthills of humanity.

He twirled the ice cubes and cursed himself. Transparent anthills of humanity. Christ. He must have poured a bigger measure than he thought. A couple of fingers of single malt at eighty proof equals pretentiousness, but pretentious or not, there was no denying the fact that he had come a long way. Hard work, vats of midnight oil burnt, ambitions achieved; self-made, pulled up by his bootstraps, from nowheresville to a million-dollar view. The problem was the pessimistic twist on the mathematical certainty that what goes up must come down, and now, as he gazed into his glass, Dean began to think of it as half empty rather than half full.

He could see the top of the tower, exactly three miles to the southwest, twenty stories of girder and green-tinted glass, standing empty. His partner Evan had dubbed it the Green Elephant, topped out the very week that Wall Street had got the jitters; designed and built in the highest hopes and expectations, and now no one would rent a square inch, and his name, etched along with Evan's and the date in gold leaf in the granite foundation stone, seemed like an epitaph.

He thought of the old Tibetan going on about emptiness. Well, the Green Elephant was empty, and if it didn't start filling up soon, we'll all be out of here, back to sea level, and the million-dollar view not even housewarmed.

He took another slug of whiskey.

"You don't drown your sorrows. You only teach them to swim."

He looked up at a reflection in the window

coming toward him and turned to see Lisa reaching for him, hugging him, taking his glass, and gulping from it. She smelt of soap.

"Where's Lama Dorje?" he said.

"Running a bath."

She handed back the glass, went across to the kitchen, and brought back the bottle. "The monks," she said. "Like the three kings from the East, huh?"

"Yeah," he said, pouring another, thinking about Dutch courage. "Amazing. At least they didn't tell us Jesse was the result of an immaculate conception."

She was watching as he drank, and he began to worry again. What if they had to move? What if his money, tied in with Evan's, was all gone? What if he had to start again? It was one thing to pick yourself up by your bootstraps once, but what if they took your boots away? What if they had to live on Lisa's salary? Could he be a house husband? He was a Self-made Man. He'd missed out on the New Man phenomenon. He sure as hell couldn't make the leap to Kept Man.

Could he?

She was looking at him drinking. Though there was no disapproval in her expression, he could not help but wonder if, when he became "kept," she would change. Would the nagging start, along with all the other horrors of married life that he had never experienced firsthand?

She was staring dreamily through the window.

"I think it's a nice idea, reincarnation," she said. "I wouldn't mind coming back. Seeing the places I like again, the people I love. . . ."

"Suppose you came back as an ant."

"What's wrong with an ant?" she said, turning back to him. "Lots of group activity."

"Sure," he said, "but you can get squashed."

Lisa looked at him, registering the gloomy response, and she knew that he was going to tell her.

"People get squashed too," she said, prompting him.

"Yeah. That's a fact."

Don't let him be ill, she said to herself. Don't let it be another woman.

"Evan's bankrupt."

The first reaction was relief, followed by disbelief. It couldn't be. Not wheeler-dealer, rich-as-Croesus Evan.

"He's been hiding it from everyone," Dean said. "Even from me."

She listened without interrupting him, stroking his hand, occasionally sipping from his glass. When he had finished, she asked him what it all meant.

He shrugged. "I don't know. If he goes under, we might lose the house."

"So? We'll be poor again." And on came the brave face, the face of an actress. "We can still be happy."

Dean squeezed her hand, and she thought maybe this hard man was about to soften and get uncharacteristically sentimental, and maybe he would have except for a call from the bathroom, an announcement from Jesse that he was ready to

43

be bathed. She got up and went to the door, then turned.

"Maybe you'll have more time to spend with us."

It was the wrong thing to say, and immediately she knew it. A man like Dean worked for time to spend with his family. He needed to earn it. Force-feed him leisure, and he would grow fat and miserable. . . .

With that thought, she pushed open the bathroom door and saw Jesse almost submerged in the tub, eyes and arms protruding. He was immersed in a book and full of questions about monks, about Tibet and Bhutan and the Himalayas.

She told him about Everest and Annapurna, and at first he did not believe they could be bigger than his Mount Rainier. She told him that the region was the roof of the world and known as Shangri-La, and when he asked what Shangri-La was, she couldn't remember whether it was real or fictional and made a note to look it up. Jesse's third-degree inquisition led inevitably to the encyclopedia.

But this was okay. The hard part was the next question.

"Mom? Is Dad angry with me?"

It was that sense of atmosphere again, as if the child were telepathic.

"No, darling. He's not upset with you. He's just got some problems, that's all."

He was satisfied, wished her good-bye, held his nose, and disappeared beneath the foam.

Lisa picked up the book and opened it to the first page. It was beautifully illustrated. Naïve art, poster paints, everything bold; the sky was azure, the buildings ocher, the saris and robes brilliant blues, reds, and greens.

Jesse popped up spluttering and peered at the court of King Suddhodana, and his lips moved as he began to read. . . .

Buddha was born two thousand five hundred years ago in northern India near the town of Kapilvista, which was named after the great hermit Kapil and had been ruled peacefully for twenty years by King Suddhodana of the Sakya race. As a prince, Suddhodana had defeated the last of his enemies, and the people now lived in peace with their neighbors and with themselves.

The town was a magical place on the roof of the world, and sometimes in the glare of the sun or the watercolor wash of the moon, it seemed somehow suspended, shimmering between earth and sky.

The castellated walls of the King's palace were now simply decoration, their ocher earthworks blending as a chameleon against the slopes of the mountain. Instead of being a scar on the land, the town complemented the contours of the mountain range.

Men, women, and children wore silk robes and saris, and the air tinkled to the sound of their bracelets, bangles, and necklaces. Everything was color, and strangers who came to visit left the place convinced that the rest of the world was gray.

The King's favorite queen was named Maya. She

was so beautiful that she had never been permitted a mirror in case she was tempted by the sin of pride. She did not know that her eyes were as black as a moonless night or that her features were in perfect symmetry. She thought that when her handmaidens looked away from her, it was out of duty and not for fear of the sin of jealousy, and that when men turned their backs, it was out of respect and not for fear of covetousness.

The palace was a honeycomb of rooms and courtyards on many levels, the walls studded with jewels and embellished with shrubs and plants. There were hanging gardens and fountains, fishponds and pools for bathing.

Peacocks strutted and swans glided, and the rose competed with the lotus to perfume the air.

The King's bedroom could be reached only by a staircase of marble threaded with gold leaf. It stretched beneath the roof of the palace of the roof of the world and was open to the elements, the bed suspended from the bamboo ceiling by ropes. It swung gently in the night breeze and violently in passion. If the Queen did not wish to see the stars or the moon, she pulled a sash and the bed was enclosed in silk curtains. The mattress was made of goose down and each night was strewn with fresh rose petals.

On the night that the man who was to be Buddha was conceived, there was a brilliant moon, but Maya had not drawn the silk. The bed was open to the sky, and it was from the heavens that, in her dream, a white elephant descended and woke her,

and she embraced it and felt as if it entered her
womb.

In the morning she told the King about the
dream, and he asked if it was a nightmare, if it had
frightened her.

"No," she said, "it was like a blessing."

And the King took her in his arms, and their
passion was fierce.

The next day the King sent for the Brahmans who
could interpret dreams, and they told him that he
would soon have a son who would become ruler of
the world. From that day on, Maya had the power
of healing. Her touch drew out pain. As she reached
out to the suffering, the blind regained their sight,
and the lame the use of their limbs, and the dying
were comforted.

Ten months passed and it was time. As was the
custom, Maya set out for her parents' village to give
birth. She traveled with her sister, Prajapati, in a
carriage drawn by two black water buffaloes. They
were escorted by foot soldiers and accompanied by
a retinue of handmaidens in a caravan of small
carriages. The monsoon was due, the air was heavy,
and lethargy blanketed the land.

The caravan traveled through flat lands of savannah grass dotted with copses of thick vegetation,
and the drivers and the buffaloes wilted in the heat
so that the progress was slow. And Maya knew that
she was not destined to reach her parents' village,
and so she called a halt at the edge of a wood which
was known as Lumbini.

For a while she prayed, knowing that it was time.
Then she was helped out of the carriage and walked

47

alone and unsteadily into the wood, her handmaidens following behind at a respectful distance. She passed between the trees and was dappled and speckled by sunlight until she reached the heart of the forest, where a canopy of intertwining vines and branches let through only single beams.

She stopped and listened to the sounds of the forest, to the chattering of monkeys, the shrieking and whistling of birds, the rustlings in the undergrowth and the gurgling of a brook. Then, as if some conductor had waved a baton, there was silence. Slowly a sapling bent toward her. She reached up and grasped it, then began to sing, and the handmaidens listened to the song of birth.

The baby boy was as large as a one year old, and gurgled happily as he was bathed in the brook, then Prajapati held him up and showed him to her sister.

Maya smiled, then gasped in astonishment as the baby slithered out of Prajapati's hands and steadied himself on his feet. For a moment he stood smiling at his mother, then he walked toward her. It took seven steps for him to reach her, and from each footprint a lotus immediately sprang and blossomed, and Maya knew that she had been truly blessed.

The King named the child Siddhartha and ordered a great feast to present him to the people. A massive bamboo pavilion was built in the fields beneath the town, and everyone in the kingdom came to pay respects to the baby Prince.

Suddhodana and Maya wore robes of silk with gold inlay and their finest jewelry. The King wore *the crown of his coronation and the Queen that of her wedding, and they sat side by side on jeweled bamboo thrones as the courtiers filed past, in silk robes of gold, maroon, green or blue, each one bowing to the thrones and murmuring blessings, the procession like an undulating snake moving between tables heavy with spices, fruits, and steaming pots of rice, past pits where pigs on spits were being roasted, past casks of wine into which gold goblets were dipped and lines of* doma *laid out to be chewed slowly to heighten the senses and sharpen the appetites.*

Outside, the multitude stood in yellow robes and turbans, row upon row of them in the fields, like a vast harvest of nodding sunflowers.

Then, at noon, the sage known as Asita arrived, and there was a sudden, respectful silence because he had not been seen for a generation. He was old now but still upright, although he leaned on a stick and moved slowly through the crowd, which parted as a river parts for a ship, each man, woman, and child dropping to make a deep bow.

Such was the reverence in which the old man was held that, when he reached the thrones, the King stood and the Queen bowed to him.

"Welcome, Asita," the King said. "You do us great honor by your visit."

The Queen handed the baby to him, and Asita, in a voice that had not spoken for many years, said that divine voices had told him that a son had been born to the King of the Sakyas and would attain true knowledge.

"He was born to you," he said, "because your

ancestors were rich in gold and land but, most of all, rich in virtue."

Asita gazed at the child and saw signs that were visible only to him, the signs of omnipotence; a tuft of blond hair between the baby's eyebrows, the mark of a wheel on the balls of his feet, thin membranes webbing his fingers, the double crown of his skull and long earlobes.

He began to sob, and the Queen, who had been studying him, suddenly snatched the baby back from him.

"Do not be alarmed," he said. "Mine are only the tears of an old man who knows that he will not live long enough to learn from the teachings of your son."

And now the King was concerned at these words of teachings and of true knowledge. He did not want Siddhartha to be a teacher. His destiny was the dynasty and its continuation.

"Will he be a great king?" he said, and the words were more a command than a question.

Asita gazed at the baby and smiled. "He will be the master of the world," he said. "Or its redeemer."

The King was confused. This was not the simple answer that he required.

"When he is old, Asita," he said, prompting the old man, "he can become a teacher like you if he wishes, but first of all he must follow me and be a king."

But Asita would not be prompted. He shook his head. "It may be as you wish, Suddhodana," he said, "but the gods often betray the wishes of mortal men."

And now the King was angry. He took the baby from his Queen and roared: "He will be king!"

And Siddhartha, startled, began to cry. The Queen reached for him, but the King stepped down from his throne and went out into the fields and held the naked child above his head, clutching him by his feet and the back of his head, and the multitude roared their approval, and such was the noise that avalanches started on the highest peaks.

As she watched, the Queen was filled with sadness as if she already knew that her own life would soon be over. A week later she was stricken with a terrible illness. She took to her bed, and the silk curtains were drawn. For two days and a night no birdsong was heard, only the drone of the city in prayer.

Suddhodana and Prajapati sat in silent vigil by her side as she prepared for death, her baby by her side.

Then, at nightfall, she looked at her sister who was but a cobweb's breath of her own beauty and compassionate nature and asked her to care for Siddhartha as if he were her own son.

And even as Prajapati made her promise, Maya died, and the candles in the room flickered out and the prayers ceased, and all that could be heard were the terrible sobs of Suddhodana and the gentle weeping of the new mother.

The story had traveled from the bathroom to the kitchen, through Jesse's supper and finally to his bed.

Lisa closed the book and kissed him goodnight.

Dean ruffled his hair and they left hand in hand, closed the door, and went into the living room.

"Strutting peacocks, gliding swans, chattering monkeys," Dean said. "Cliché heaped upon cliché."

"Sure," Lisa said, "but we're talking five hundred years B.C. here. Clichés weren't clichés then."

"And an elephant?"

"So? The virgin Mary had her angel. This is legend, Dean. Mythology. Didn't you read Hesse at college?"

"Who's Hesse?"

"Hermann. You know. *Siddhartha. Steppenwolf.*"

"Steppenwolf was a band."

She smiled. He was kidding again, playing the role of the down-to-earth, self-made man again with no time for arty-farty literature, and suddenly, and irresistibly, it was time for bed.

Four

Chompa had always been known for the power of his imagination, but nothing that he had anticipated about America had prepared him for this thing known as a monorail, this sealed tube of metal, traveling along a single track at, Jesse had told him, thirty miles an hour, fifty feet from the ground, swooping and bending between the buildings, above the traffic, sometimes seeming to be going through the great glass buildings before swerving aside, then diving between towering canyons of concrete.

His smile was stitched across his face in a pretense of enjoyment because it would not do to show fear in front of the boy, but his eyes betrayed him. His eyes did not smile. They stared at one spot, and his knuckles, grasping the seat in front of him, looked like lines of pebbles. Now and again he glanced at Lama Norbu and drew strength from him. The old man was looking around him, as curious as a child, and Chompa told himself that if he was unafraid, then there was nothing to worry about.

The machine erupted out of a canyon into brilliant sunshine and ran for a while alongside the bay, and Chompa looked behind to see how the dark-haired woman was taking it. Maria smiled at him as if to comfort him, and he felt better, knowing that she, who seemed like a stranger here, was unafraid. But why did they need to go so fast?

Jesse would know, and Chompa, as he asked, felt like the child with Jesse as the adult.

"This isn't fast," Jesse said, as if it were a dumb question. "Wait till you go on a roller coaster."

Whatever a roller coaster was, Chompa wanted nothing to do with it. Then Jesse was pointing and bouncing on his seat. "Look, look. That green building over there. See? My dad designed that. He's an architect. His name's on the stone."

"Very good," the Lama said. "He must be very clever."

"The best," Jesse said. Then he poked the old man in the chest. "I know why you're here," the boy said. "You're looking for your teacher, aren't you?"

How did he know? Chompa wondered. Was this some form of precognition? But the old man just smiled.

"Yes," he said. "And red rats have very big ears."

Ah. That was it. The boy had been eavesdropping.

"What's his name?" Jesse asked.

The Lama told him: "Lama Dorje, which means thunderbolt in your language."

"Yeah?" Jesse said, impressed. Thunderbolt. He'd like to be called Jesse Thunderbolt. It was a better name than Konrad.

"It was a good name for him. He had a very powerful mind. Always making jokes."

"Does he smell funny like you?"

Chompa smiled. The little boy wasn't quite as smart as he seemed. He hadn't picked up on the past tense, but then again, why should he? He simply assumed that they must be looking for someone living in the city.

The Lama was laughing at the question.

"That must be the smell of yak butter," he said. "We use so much of it that the smell gets into our skin."

"What's a yak?"

"A Tibetan cow. Like a buffalo with long hair."

Jesse nodded, then frowned. "I think you should go to the police if you want to find him," he said.

"No," Lama Norbu said. "The police can't help us, I'm afraid. You see, Lama Dorje is dead."

Jesse stared at him. "But how can you find him if he's dead?"

"It's difficult to explain, but we think he has been reborn."

Jesse whistled and glanced at Maria, who was gazing incredulously at the old man. This was great, Jesse thought. This was better than stories about yaks.

"Like a ghost you mean?"

"No. As a child."

Jesse digested this and leaned forward so that his face was only an inch from the Lama's nose.

"Could I be Lama Dorje?"

Maria, watching, expected the man to laugh and say "Don't be silly," but he remained serious.

"You could be. Yes," he said, and Maria had to look away so that she wouldn't burst out laughing, which would have been ill-mannered and unforgivable in front of strangers.

Jesse tugged at his left ear for a moment, then nodded. "I think I am," he said. "I am Lama Dorje."

The old man smiled. "We'll have to see about that," he said.

"Then if I'm not, why did you come to our house."

Perfectly logical, Maria thought, and the old man could not answer it. Instead, he just laughed, tweaked Jesse's nose, and said, "You ask a lot of questions."

Jesse was disappointed. It was like when he was younger and when his mom and dad were stumped and they just said, "Because. . . ."

He was about to press home his advantage when Maria leaned forward and whispered a suggestion. It was a good one. He wished he'd thought of it himself.

"Yes, Maria, yes," he said and clenched his fists

in triumph. He would show them. He would show them where the Buddha lived.

Ten minutes later Jesse led the little procession into the museum and up to the first floor and pointed triumphantly. The ten-foot statue sat in the lotus position in front of a wall of glass with the Seattle skyline as a background.

Chompa stared at it in astonishment, amazed that nonbelievers in the West had gone to the trouble to give the Buddha pride of place in their city. It showed tolerance and compassion for the beliefs of others. These were not narrow-minded people. Indeed, he thought, they are more open than we are, for there were no statues to the man they called Jesus in Bhutan.

They stood in silence for a while, and it was Jesse who broke the spell.

"Was Buddha a god?" he asked, looking into the smiling stone face.

"No," the Lama said, "he was a real person."

"Like Jesus?" Jesse continued, pulling a book from his backpack.

"Yes. Quite a bit like Jesus, although he was born long before."

"Siddhartha's a funny name."

"In your language," the Lama said, "it means he-who-brings-good."

They moved along the corridor and came to a bas-relief of Queen Maya with the elephant, and Jesse frowned.

"Why did she have to die? I didn't like that bit."

The old man knelt before him and took the boy's hands in his big right hand.

"But life is not all happiness," he said. "That is what Siddhartha had come to teach us. How to see beyond life and death."

He took the book from Jesse and opened it. . . .

He grew up straight, handsome, and strong, and lived, according to the seasons, in one of three palaces—one for summer, one for winter, one for the rainy season. And he never saw the world outside. He traveled from one to the other in a carriage without windows and did not think it odd. He assumed that everyone traveled in such a manner.

When it came time for him to marry, the King invited all the young girls of the city to the palace. Siddhartha sat on a golden throne in the main courtyard, flanked by statues of the great elephant. His handmaidens had dressed him in a simple robe and forsworn any jewelry for fear that the women would be overcome by the sight of him. Like his mother, he had never seen a mirror; like her he did not know that his eyes were as black as a moonless night or that his features were in perfect symmetry. He took no pride in the perfection of his sun-blessed body, lithe and tightly muscled from daily sport, and he accepted that he was the strongest and the fastest simply because he was the Prince and such excellence was ordained. Having never known defeat, he knew nothing of competition and accepted without question that his bride would be the wisest and most beautiful woman in the land.

They formed a line and, as they came up to him,

58

he gave each one a jewel. Such was his beauty that none dared look at him. Each one took the gift with lowered eyes and moved away.

The last was named Yasodhara and immediately Siddhartha knew that she was the one.

She looked straight into his eyes, and he reached for a jewel, but there was none left, except for a ring that he was wearing. He took it off and offered it to her, but she declined and said that it was for her to give him something, not to take from him.

The King saw and heard this and summoned her father to the palace and asked him to give Yasodhara as a bride to his son, but the man was a proud Sakyan and refused. His daughter would marry a brave, wise, and skilled man, not one who had lived a life of indolence and had never been put to the test.

Far from being offended, the King organized a series of contests to which every young man was invited and Yasodhara's father promised her to the one who excelled overall.

The first test was in the art of writing. One young man who thought himself skilled came forward, but the teacher Visvamitra told him that Siddhartha, as a child, already knew sixty-four varieties of script and the young man went away abashed.

Then came the mathematics tests, which lasted no time at all as Siddhartha answered correctly, even before any of the problems were finished being put to him.

The contest turned to the athletic arena, where he won every race and jumped the highest. And in the wrestling matches known as kabadi, *he was again supreme, throwing every opponent to the sand.*

Finally there was an archery contest. At first he could not compete; such was his strength that he broke every bow, and so the King sent for an ancient bow that had been displayed for centuries in the temple. No man had ever been able to draw it, but Siddhartha did so with one finger. The target was painted on a tree so far away that none but he could see it, and when he fired, the arrow split the trunk and buried itself in the ground where a well sprung up and was from then on known as the Well of the Arrow.

And so Yasodhara's father gave his daughter to Siddhartha. The wedding feast lasted for ten days and nights, and for months afterward they led a life of pleasure in which every sense was sharp and every appetite whetted.

Yasodhara became pregnant, and the birth was imminent when the first mistakes were made, and Siddhartha heard the first words of the new language.

It was after a wrestling match in front of the court. Siddhartha had led his team to victory, defeating the team led by his charioteer, whose name was Channa.

They left the arena and walked past a flower bed. A gardener was changing the flowers and the gods made Siddhartha notice and ask the man what he was doing. The man replied that he was putting in new ones, and Siddhartha asked why.

"You know the way your father is," the gardener

said in all innocence. "He likes the flowers to be changed before they wither."

"'Wither'?" Siddhartha said. "What is 'wither'?"

The gardener could only smile because he was unable to explain to Siddhartha the meaning of death.

"'Wither'?" Siddhartha said again and laughed as Yasodhara distracted him, and for the moment the word went out of his mind.

The crisis had passed, but not for long. It was noon on midsummer's day when the first doubt arrived on the scented air as if by accident.

Siddhartha was lying on a couch in the courtyard, half asleep. One handmaiden massaged his feet with oils. Another tended to the nails of his left hand. Yasodhara sat nearby on silk cushions. Peacocks, as they strutted past, spread their tail feathers in respect. The sound of a girl singing and playing a sitar drifted across the courtyard, and Siddhartha opened his eyes. It was the strangest, most beautiful sound he had heard, a song of joy but sung as if in sadness, although Siddhartha did not know the meaning of the word. Had he heard of melancholy, he would have recognized the emotion, but to him, it was only strange.

He got up and walked to the parapet where the girl was singing and looked up at her. He cocked his head like a curious puppy; then Yasodhara was at his side, and he asked her what the song was. As if tricked by a mischievous god, she in turn made a mistake. She told him that it was a song from a faraway land about the wonder and the beauties of *the country where the girl came from and the lakes and mountains she could not forget.*

"How strange," he said. "Do such places exist? As beautiful as here?" The idea seemed inconceivable. "I have never wanted to go outside."

Yasodhara sensed that she had stimulated a dangerous curiosity in him, and she attempted to nip it in the bud.

"I have heard that only suffering lies beyond these walls," she said and immediately realized that she had made a second mistake. He turned to her and said, "What is suffering?"

She sighed and looked away. "Your father loves you very much," she said. "He has given us everything you could want. There is no need to go anywhere else when you have such beauty around you."

"It is true," Siddhartha said. "We have everything, and everything is perfect. So what is this feeling I have? If the world is so beautiful, why have I never seen it? I haven't even seen my own city. I must see the world, with my own eyes."

And Yasodhara began to weep and turned away from him, realizing that this new curiosity was a danger to them both.

He wanted to see the world—whatever that was.

The room was silent, the atmosphere a fog of concentration. Lisa was at her desk, compiling an exam paper; Dean on the sofa, studying a design. Downstairs the door opened, and Lisa smiled. She had been growing anxious, wondering why Maria had kept Jesse out so long. She had been making up newspaper headlines about a Seattle boy abducted by Tibetan monks, seeing herself on CNN saying on camera that they had seemed so nice, as the viewers sniggered about her gullibility. But everything was okay now. He was back. She could hear Maria chattering, then the sound of his footsteps on the stairs, and she wondered if there was something wrong because normally he bounded, goatlike; now he was trudging, like his father after a hard day, and when he looked in, he was anxious.

"Mom, if you die, will you come back?"

God. What a question.

"What are you talking about, Jesse? I'm not going to die."

"Everybody dies."

Then she realized. The book. The death of the Queen. Time to change the subject.

"How was Lama Norbu?" she asked, and at the sound of the man's name, Jesse beamed.

"He was great." He skipped up to Dean. "I showed him your building, Dad."

"Good."

"And, Dad, Lama Dorje means Lama Thunderbolt. And Bhutan is the land of the thunder dragon." He picked up the brass bell from the coffee table and swung it. "And I want to go there. I want to go to the land of the thunder dragon."

That decided, Jesse left the room, taking giant steps, tinkling the bell and muttering "thunderbolt" over and over like a litany.

Lisa turned and saw Dean gazing at her, his head to one side, looking thoughtful.

"Why are you looking at me like that?" she asked.

"Like what?"

"Like you never saw me before."

"It's my Tibetan look."

Huh? Tibetan look? It was unlike Dean to be enigmatic.

"What?"

"I mean, this is all fine and dandy," he said slowly. "But how far do we want to go with it?"

Lisa shrugged.

"The reincarnation of Jesse Konrad," he said, heavy with sarcasm. "You know your son, don't you?"

She wasn't having that. How dare he patronize her? Of course, she knew her son. She'd brought him up for eight years. She was about to tell him so, but Dean kept on talking.

"You know what kind of imagination he's got. He's going to get confused. Isn't he?"

She shrugged again. She didn't see anything wrong with the exercise. The Siddhartha book was stimulating. It was a damned sight better for Jesse than computer games.

"And upset," he persisted. "I tell you—soon he's gonna start thinking that he is Lama Dorje." Then he smiled. "That's supposed to be a joke."

But she wasn't laughing. "Maybe," she said. "But how often does a little boy from Seattle get to learn about another world? It's like a fairy tale come true."

"Except that it's not true, is it?" He had become suddenly angry. "I don't believe in reincarnation.

Not like this, anyway. Coming back as a specific person with a name, address, and telephone number. And neither do you."

He was expecting an answer, demanding that she agree with him, but she said nothing.

"Or do you?" he insisted.

"No."

"So?"

She could not look at him. She stared instead at a pile of exercise books. The name on the cover was the bright kid, the one who would go all the way. Dean wanted reassurance from her. He wanted her to back up his skepticism, but she couldn't do it. She kept seeing the face of the old man and hearing the dignity in his voice. To agree with Dean would somehow mean betraying the Lama, and she could not bring herself to do it.

"We don't know much about anything," she said. "And absolutely nothing about the most important things of all. We don't know why we were born. Or if there is a why."

She looked up and dared him to contradict her, to contradict the great why-are-we-here? question that none of the biggest brains on the planet had answered.

"And that's interesting," she said.

Dean sighed, held up his hands, palms forward in a gesture of surrender.

"I've gotta call Evan," he said.

He had bankruptcy to discuss. Reincarnation could be put on hold.

Five

"Just what I always wanted." As she drove downtown, she heard again the sarcasm in his voice—a nastiness that was new to him. And then yesterday, his barely concealed anger. He had always been a bit of a skeptic, a down-to-earth kind of guy, which was okay, but there was a fine line between skepticism and cynicism, between wit and vitriol, and she hoped that the worry wasn't taking him over that line, because she did not want to live with a world-weary cynic. That wasn't part of the deal when they had made their vows. . . .

"Left," Jesse yelled. "No, right. No, left."

"Make up your—"

"Yeah, left, that's it. Look. Over there."

She'd seen the place before. A vaulted clapboard building that had once been a Methodist church. She remembered the congregation coming out on Sunday morning as she had walked past in the drizzle; they had worn gray suits and black hats. Now the Buddhists had given it a coat of cream paint, and the words *Dharma Center* stood out in maroon above the door.

"What's 'dharma' mean, Mom?"

"I think it means 'the way' or something," she said, gesturing in the air with her fingers to indicate the quotation marks. Her parents had gone through a beatnik phase before she was born, and one of the reminders was a book by Kerouac called *The Dharma Bums*. She had tried to read it, but it hadn't claimed her. She was the wrong generation.

She pulled up, and Jesse was out quickly, his book in his right hand. He was getting, she thought, to be like a commercial for Amex: He never left home without it.

Chompa turned and bowed as they came in, and Lisa looked around approvingly. Gone was the austerity and grimness of the Methodists with their hard pews and bleak exhortations about the fear of God. This was a colorful place of celebration. The pulpit was gone and was replaced by scaffolding. Two painters were working on an image of the Buddha.

The other walls were covered with paintings.

"We call these *tankas*," Chompa said. "And the white scarf we offer as a greeting is called a *kata*."

"Okay," Lisa said, and stood listening to the monotone of the monks at their devotions.

"That is the Heart Sutra," he said. "It's our most famous prayer."

"Like the Lord's Prayer!"

"I expect so."

They walked up to the scaffolding and listened as Chompa translated the monks' murmurings: "Form is emptiness . . . emptiness is form . . . All things are emptiness, not born, not destroyed. . . . No eye, ear, nose, tongue, body, mind . . . No color, sound, smell, taste, touch, existing thing."

Then he smiled and looked embarrassed. "It is difficult to translate so quickly."

"It's beautiful," Lisa said and checked her watch. "But I have to leave." She ruffled Jesse's hair and knelt in front of him. "Dad will pick you up at four. Okay?"

He nodded and turned back to gaze at the Buddha, and she walked away. At the door she turned and looked at him, the little blond boy among all these chanting men in maroon and stifled a tremor of apprehension.

He would be okay here, wouldn't he? Just for an hour or so? Better with these people than with the Methodists with their grim view of the world and their fear of God.

He'd be okay. It was only an hour.

Chompa waved as she left, then he led Jesse to a room at the back of the church. The word *Vestry* was painted in gold leaf. He knocked and waited but there was no answer; he eased the door open and stepped inside on tiptoe.

It was a small room, just a narrow bed, a wooden altar, and a small dressing table. On the altar stood the photograph of Lama Dorje.

Lama Norbu sat cross-legged on the bed, his rosary twisted around his fingers. His head was slumped to one side. Quickly Chompa went up to him and bent an ear to his chest. As he did so, the old man sat up and blinked.

"Excuse me," Chompa said. "I was worried."

"One day, Chompa," the old man said, "but not yet." Then he looked beyond him to the door where Jesse was standing. The old man beckoned to him to come in, and the boy went straight to the altar.

"Hey, that's Lama Thunderbolt," he said.

"That's right."

The two men exchanged a glance as the boy gazed at the photograph. Then he went to the dressing table. A thermos flask and two cups stood next to four wooden bowls. Three were new, the fourth old and cracked. Jesse picked up the old one and frowned, then muttered irritably, "It's dusty." And rubbed it clean on his elbow.

Again the two men looked at each other, and Chompa thought, Maybe it's just coincidence, and maybe he just guessed that the photo was Lama Dorje.

Maybe.

Now Jesse was picking up something that had been hidden behind the bowls. He held it up and looked at the old man for an answer.

"It's a trumpet made of human bones."

"Honest?" His eyes looked like golf balls. He

raised it to his lips and blew. The trumpet shrieked, and Jesse giggled. The old man took the book from him and opened it.

"So," he said. "What have you learned?"

"Siddhartha wanted to see the world."

Jesse hopped onto the bed as the old man found the page, and as he started to read, Chompa watched and was reminded of the boy monks at home, of snakes and a mongoose. . . .

The King knew that the time had come and he could not delay the inevitable. Siddhartha was, as the ancient saying had it, like an elephant too long confined in his stable. It was the most luxurious of stables, but since Yasodhara had unwittingly spoken, Siddhartha saw it as stable locked from within, and he went to his father and told him that he was preparing to leave, to go on a great journey.

The King had anticipated this day and had prepared for it. The old, the sick, and the beggars were rounded up and taken far from the route of the procession. Siddhartha would see the world outside, see that it was as happy and cheerful as the palace grounds, and his itch of curiosity would disappear. He would be content to follow his father and be King. The dynasty would continue, and that was all that mattered.

The day came. Siddhartha was twenty-nine years old. Maidens bathed him and oiled his body. His long black hair, which had never seen a blade, was teased and contoured into ringlets, and they dressed him in a blue-and-gold robe, then placed a crown on him, and hung a jeweled necklace of six medal-

lions on his chest. A diamond-studded bracelet was snapped onto his left forearm, and his right hand was encrusted with rings.

When he appeared in the courtyard, men cheered and women sighed.

Channa was waiting for him. He wore a simple red cloak and held Siddhartha's white stallion, Kantaka, by the reins. Siddhartha smiled at him and said, "We are going to see the world." Then he was helped onto a palanquin, the throne of mahogany, inlaid with gold leaf. A canopy of peacock feathers protected him from the noonday sun.

He looked up at the balcony and waved at his father, his aunt, and at Yasodhara, who, he thought, must have caught some dirt in her eye because she was rubbing her face as if trying not to cry. Then the King gave a signal. Trumpets blared, drums beat a tattoo, and the palanquin was lifted onto the shoulders of three dozen men in yellow robes.

The trumpets died away, and the drums beat out a rhythm to guide the footsteps of the bearers. Siddhartha looked down at Channa and beamed with anticipation, then the massive gates were dragged open, and he saw the world.

It was a narrow street, a canyon of houses three stories high and studded at each window with a balcony, the wood freshly painted red, ocher, and yellow. A mass of people lined the streets, leaned out of windows and balconies, and squatted on the rooftops. There was no space anywhere that was not taken up by men, women, and children in their best robes and turbans.

Every face smiled at him from below and above, and as he left the palace, he was showered with rose petals and red powder so that he could barely see. For a moment the drums ceased, and the crowd, in unison, roared out his name, each one as rehearsed emphasizing the second syllable: "See-DAAAAR-ta! See-DAAAAR-ta! See-DAAAR-ta." The drums took up the rhythm. The air was a blizzard of rose petals. Siddhartha grabbed handfuls, smelt them, threw them toward a pretty girl, then stood and held out his arms as if to embrace the whole world.

"SEE-DAAAR-TA! SEE-DAAAAR-TA! SEE-DAAAAR-TA . . ."

And the word that Yasodhara had used which had so upset him vanished from his memory.

He remained on his feet as the palanquin was carried slowly along the street. Every face to left and right, below and above, smiled and shouted his name; hands reached out to him, but he could not reach them. He was in ecstasy, and he wished this moment would not stop, but he could see the end of the world now, a hundred yards away. He would be carried to it. Then, as rehearsed, the throne would be swiveled around on its bearings, and the men would raise the palanquin from their shoulders, turn around, and head back to the palace. Siddhartha was already anticipating the feasting and the dancing when he saw the monsters.

There was an alley to his left. It was empty as he glanced at it, then he looked up at a young girl who was holding out her arms to him, and when he looked away from her, the two monsters had appeared in the mouth of the alley. Siddhartha stif-

fened and stared at them. They were more or less shaped like men, but what little hair they had was the color of Kantaka's mane, and at first he thought that they were bending to pick something up, but they did not straighten, just stood bent and seemingly broken. Their skin was wrinkled and their ribs stood out like the spokes on the fans that cooled him in the noon sun. Then they saw him and smiled, and they had only three teeth between them, teeth like little tusks, yellow and cracked. Siddhartha closed his eyes and thought for a moment that he must be dreaming one of those dreams that Yasodhara had tried to describe as a nightmare, whatever that was, and when he opened his eyes, he saw two guards lift the monsters from behind as if they weighed no more than puppies and carry them away down the alley, their thin arms waving like drumsticks.

Channa would know. Channa had been born on the Outside. He bent toward him and pointed.

"Who are these, men?" he said, wondering indeed if they were men.

"Men like the rest of us, my lord," Channa said. "Men who sucked at their mothers' breasts."

"But why do they look that way?"

And Channa made a mistake. "Because they are old, my lord."

Another strange syllable, another meaningless sound.

"What do you mean? 'Old'?"

"Old age destroys memory, beauty, and strength," Channa said, compounding his error, and he knew *he should not answer, but his tongue did not obey his brain. "In the end it happens to us all, my lord."*

It was said. It was done. The words were out, and Siddhartha was staring at him; then he shook his head as if trying to shake away the memory of "old," but another word crept in uninvited.

"Withered."

"Withered," "old," "suffering." New words. Terrible words, and suddenly, without warning, he leaped from the palanquin into the crowd. It was so unexpected that Channa stood motionless for a moment before handing the reins to a guard. At first he thought he had lost the Prince and thanked the gods for the gold crown that bobbed up among the crowd, then disappeared as Siddhartha turned into the alleyway. Channa, pushing through the crowd, was panicking now, for if the unthinkable happened, if he lost the Prince, he could not imagine the King's wrath and what it might mean. . . .

Then Channa found him, at the end of the alley, which gave into a large square. He was staring at another old man, his head cocked curiously, just staring and sniffing. Channa ran up to him, and Siddhartha turned, then pointed to the old man.

"Does this happen to everyone?" he asked.

Channa nodded.

"To you?"

He nodded again.

"To me?"

"It is better not to concern yourself with these things, my lord," Channa said, but even as he said the words, he knew he was wasting breath and tried to imagine the shock that was convulsing Sid-

dhartha's brain—his first intimation of mortality, and at twenty-nine years of age. What would he do? How would he react? Siddhartha's response was a surprise. He took off his jewelry and his crown, handed them to Channa, then told him to give him his robe. Right there in a filthy alleyway with an open sewer running through, the great Prince of the Sakyas disrobed and stood naked for a moment until Channa handed over his robe. Siddhartha put it on, covered his head with the cowl, and turned toward the square, leaving Channa to follow in his loincloth, clutching the gold-and-blue robe and the richest jewels in the land.

Siddhartha walked slowly into the square and looked around. This was the world. This was no procession route. People were going about their business unconcerned with this stranger in a red cloak. No one paid him any heed. It was the first time in his life that he had felt invisible.

He watched fascinated as men forked bales of straw onto carts. A potter worked at his wheel. Other men stood on grinding wheels, whipping them into frenzied motion. Channa came up to him and Siddhartha asked what they were doing.

"Grinding corn," Channa said.

"Why?"

"To make bread."

He had never thought that bread had to be made. To him it was something that was served up, with the wine.

He crossed the square, looking at people in stalls selling fruit and meat, and he was cursed at for the

*first time in his life when he bumped into a man
carrying kindling; but he did not take offense for he
did not know what the man was saying. He wandered to his right and to his left with Channa
behind him, then stopped as he heard a terrible
wailing. He walked toward it, up two tiers of mud
steps and across an evil-smelling stream to a hut
with a thatched roof. The noise grew in intensity as
he approached, and at first it sounded to him as
Yasodhara sometimes sounded in passion, but
when he looked inside, he saw the opposite of what
he was expecting. An old woman lay on a straw
mattress, her face ravaged and swollen. His nostrils
were offended by the smell, and he pinched them
with two fingers. Then the woman coughed horri-
bly and spat an obscenity into the dirt floor.*

*Siddhartha was frightened, and it was a new
sensation for he had never known fear.*

*"What is the matter with her?" he said. "Why is
she moaning like that?"*

"She is in pain, my lord. She is very sick."

*No, he thought. Pain was when you were hurt at
kabadi. It went away quickly. It wasn't a problem.
And this other new word—"sick."*

*He looked beyond at yet more monsters lying on
straw. People with terrible, disfigured faces, some
with pieces of their bodies missing. They
looked . . . "withered."*

Was "withered" the same as "sick"?

He turned to Channa again and asked.

"Perhaps it is better not to know," Channa said.

*And Siddhartha got angry. This again was some-
thing new, Channa refusing to answer him.*

77

"Tell me," he said. "I command you."

Channa looked away and spoke so quietly and reluctantly that Siddhartha had to strain to hear.

"Sickness is a misfortune common to all creatures. No one reaches the moment of death without falling ill at least once."

"Even kings?" His voice was incredulous.

Channa's silence was an eloquent answer.

Siddhartha looked away from him. Four men, naked but for loincloths and yellow turbans, were carrying a large box on their shoulders and intoning a mantra that Siddhartha had never heard, a sound like the lowing of water buffaloes.

"And death?" he said, turning back to Channa. "What moment is that?"

Channa merely shrugged and looked at the ground.

"Show me, Channa," Siddhartha said. "It is too late to go back. Show me death."

And Channa knew he had no choice.

Slowly he led Siddhartha out of the square and down a narrow street of rotting houses until they came to a river. A silent crowd of old men and women lay along its banks.

"This is where they wait," Channa said.

Fires were burning. The sun was fierce, and the smell of something being cooked made Siddhartha feel hungry. At the riverbank he saw a wooden platform covered with sticks and branches and something white lying on it, some kind of enormous bird, Siddhartha thought, motionless in its nest.

As they drew nearer, smoke and grit got in their

eyes. They stopped to rub their eyes clear, and the four men with the box passed them. Siddhartha watched, his head cocked again like a puppy, as the white bird was lifted from its nest and it looked as though it was in human form, like a large baby in swaddling clothes. Then the men with the box reached the nest and took another creature in white from the box and placed it on the nest.

Siddhartha shook his head to try and clear the confusion, but everywhere he looked was mystery.

An old man stood knee-deep in the green river and laid a bowl in the water. Siddhartha walked to the banks and saw it float past. It was filled with ashes.

Then Channa was at his side, pointing to the white bundle lying a few feet away, near one of the fires, and Siddhartha saw now that it was human. Its feet were in the river, and a priest was intoning a mantra over it.

"This is death, my lord," Channa whispered.

And still Siddhartha did not comprehend, not until the body in the shroud was lifted, and even then he could not believe what the men were doing—that they were placing it on a nest of wood and leaves—not until a man with a torch lit the nest and it exploded in flame.

"Death is the moment of separation which comes to every person," Channa was saying. "Everyone, in every family. When a body grows cold and stiff like wood, then its life is ended and it has to be burned like wood."

Siddhartha moved closer to the pyre, and as he watched, a holy man in a loincloth squatted next to

79

him. Siddhartha did not notice him. All he could see was the burning. All he could smell was the roasting. He saw fat ooze from the burning shroud and drip into the embers. He saw the face become a skull, the body become a branch of ribs, and he did not notice Channa leave or the sun go down or the day become night.

Finally the fires were out and the people had gone, and only he and the holy man remained. Siddhartha reached out and gathered a handful of warm ashes, then he got to his feet and walked back toward the square and along the filthy alley to the street, which was still carpeted with rose petals.

Once inside the palace he did something that he had never done. He entered his father's courtyard unannounced and saw him seated by a pool, saw a handmaiden dying his beard, saw that the beard which had not yet been dyed was as white as Kantaka's mane. And now he knew that what Channa had said was true, that these new words applied even to kings and even to himself, that one day he would become that which he clutched in his hand, and the knowledge made him angry.

The King, as he saw him, tried to cover his beard, but even as he did so, he knew that it was too late and that all his preparations had been in vain.

"Oh, my father," Siddhartha said. "Why have you hidden the truth from me for so long? Why have you lied to me about the existence of poverty, death, and old age?"

"If I have lied to you, it has been because I love you."

"No." Siddhartha shook his head violently. "Can

love be dressed in lies? Your love has become a prison. How can I live as I lived before, when so many are suffering outside?"

"You never wanted to go outside." Even as he spoke, the King knew that the response was feeble.

"I must leave this palace of illusions, Father," Siddhartha said. "I must find an end to suffering."

The King had one final hope, something that would be news to his son.

"Even if you betray me," he asked, "have you no pity for the wife you leave and . . . for your son?"

Siddhartha beamed at him.

"My child is born?" he said.

"This very evening. Think of them."

But Siddhartha's smile faded, and he turned away, his mind full of confusion. The King came up to him and gently laid his hand on Siddhartha's shoulder.

"You too are a father," he said. "You too have a duty. You cannot leave now."

Siddhartha slowly shook his head, and for a moment the King thought that the Prince was agreeing with him, that he was admitting that he could not go, but when he turned, the King saw the fire of resolution in his eyes.

"Even my love for Yasodhara and my son cannot remove the pain I feel," he said sadly. "For I know that they too will have to grow old and die. Like you, like me, like all of us."

And he reached for his father's hand and smeared it with ashes.

The King shuddered and drew back in revulsion.

"Yes," he said softly. "We must all die and be reborn and die again. No man can ever escape that curse."

"Then that curse is my task," Siddhartha said. "I will lift that curse."

He turned and walked out. The King went to the fountain and washed the ashes of humanity from his hand, then shouted to the guards at his door. "Lock the gates. Double the guard. If the Prince tries to leave the palace, he must be stopped by force."

The man who would be Buddha was a prisoner in his own home.

Lama Norbu closed the book, and Jesse blinked, came out of a trance, and turned to see his father leaning against the door. He yelled Dad and ran to him.

Dean asked if he was interrupting, and the old man shook his head. Jesse showed him the trumpet. Dean said wow, patted the little boy's head, and told him that he wanted a quiet word with Lama Norbu. Chompa took Jesse by the hand and said he'd show him around, and the two men were left alone.

"I was just telling Jesse the story of—"

"I know," Dean said. "I was listening. It's a beautiful story. A beautiful myth."

"It's a way of telling the truth. Children seem to love it."

Dean nodded. "Lama Norbu," he said. "I have a great respect for your religion and your culture. I know about the invasion of Tibet and the tragedy that happened and I—"

"But you are frightened," the Lama said.

Dean smiled, relieved. He had thought that what he was about to say might get messy, might lead to an argument—two men of different cultures, from different generations, with no referee or translator—but the man seemed to be a bit of a mind reader and the very soul of tolerance.

"I am in a way," he said. "I mean, I don't want to be like Siddhartha's father. I don't want to protect Jesse from the outside world, wrap him in cotton wool, or anything, but—"

"It is natural to protect the people you love," the Lama said. "Sometimes the truth is painful."

Right, Dean thought. You said it. Now let's get this over with.

"Lama Norbu," he said. "I don't believe in reincarnation and neither does my wife."

There. It was said. Now for the argument, now for the attempt at conversion. Now the old man was gonna come on like a Moonie or a goddamn fundamentalist preacher. Instead, the Lama smiled his gentle smile and nodded in agreement.

"Why should you?" he said. "According to the Buddha, you shouldn't believe in anything unless you test it like gold." He reached for the thermos flask and offered Dean a cup of tea. Dean shook his head. The old man picked up the flask, poured himself a cup, and held it up for inspection.

"In Tibet we think of the mind and the body like the contents and the container," he said.

He banged the cup on the table. Dean twitched, startled. The cup lay in pieces, and tea began to drip onto the floor.

"The cup is no longer a cup," the old man said. "But what is the tea?"

"It's still tea," Dean said.

"Exactly. In the cup, on the table, on the floor. It moves from one container to another, but it's still tea. Like the mind after death, it moves from one body to another, but it is still mind." He reached across to the bed and took a small washcloth from the sheet, wiped up the puddle, smiled up at Dean.

"Even in the washcloth," he said. "It's still the same tea."

Dean grinned back at him. A neat allusion. But, as in all religious parables, it proved nothing. You still needed blind faith.

The old man nodded toward the photograph.

"At the end of his life," he said, "Lama Dorje came to the West. He felt the Dharma was needed everywhere in the world. This perhaps is the spiritual purpose of the Tibetan exile. He died in this house."

A memory surfaced, of a phone call to Lisa.

"March first, right? Six-thirty in the morning."

The Lama smiled. "That's correct. And so, because he came here, we thought he might choose to be reborn in the West."

"You can choose how you are going to be reborn?" Dean gaped at him. The man piled surprise upon surprise.

"A great spirit, yes, but it is still very hard for us to identify him."

"And suppose you do? What happens to that person?"

"There are no definite rules. Normally the child would receive a special education in one of our great monasteries. He could become a powerful figure in our society—a spiritual leader."

Dean glanced over his shoulder. At the door he could see Jesse talking to Chompa.

"Even as a Westerner?" he asked, turning back. "I mean, are you offering Jesse a life in a Buddhist monastery? Is that it?"

"Of course. If you wanted it. Or he could go on with his life here and decide when he is older. You see, all this is almost as new to us as it is to you. It is really very rare. It's very funny, too."

He was laughing again. Dean stared at him. He didn't get the joke, but he knew one thing, that any preconceptions he had about Buddhist monks were false. If he had thought about them at all, he would have had them down as serious and austere, forever in a trance of meditation, but this bunch seemed to find everything a laugh. And it was infectious. Dean found himself smiling along with the Lama; then the old man coughed and grew serious once more.

"To be sure of reincarnation," he said, "we would have to take Jesse to Bhutan to consult the Abbot of the monastery and other experts."

Dean's smile died on him.

"Now you look angry," the Lama said.

"I am," Dean said. "Taking children away from their families. In this country we call it kidnapping."

Lama Norbu shook his head and was about to reply when Jesse ran into the room, going *vroom-*

vroom, riding an imaginary motorbike. He was carrying an envelope and he handed it to the Lama. "Special delivery for Lama Norbu," he said and *vroomed* out again.

The Lama slit the envelope with his thumb and said, "We would hope that you and your wife would come with him."

"To Bhutan?" Dean said. He didn't even know where the damned place was.

"It is a very beautiful country," the old man said as he read. Then he looked up.

"Though perhaps the problem won't arise. It seems our search has been complicated by the appearance of another candidate. A little boy living in Kathmandu."

"Well," Dean said, "he has my total support." He paused. "Lama Norbu, I think you should go back to your world and let us stay here in ours, where I've got enough problems as it is."

He turned to go and saw Jesse at the door, looking past him at the old man and Dean felt as if he didn't even exist.

"Are there a lot of us Lama Norbu?" he asked. "How many are there? I wanna meet them."

Dean had had enough of all this. His son was more interested in the old fraud than in him. He roughly lifted him up. It was time to go. The old man painfully heaved himself off the bed, picked up the book, and hobbled after them. Jesse called out to him over his father's shoulder.

"Your book, Jesse . . ." he shouted, reaching for him, handing it to him as Dean turned and stalked off, and they could hear his voice plaintively crying: "Good-bye, Jesse Long-Ears."

The boy went rigid in Dean's arms, and Dean said good-bye without turning. And he meant good-bye—not farewell or see-you or *hasta mañana*. Good-bye. For keeps.

They drove in silence, father and son, Dean's hands tight-knuckled on the wheel. He knew his anger was a jealous pique, and the knowledge merely reinforced the problem. So the old boy was a nice guy? So what? So he played games with teacups? So he gave presents to strangers? So he'd come halfway around the world to see Jesse? So what? The very notion of traveling to the Himalayas was absurd. How could the old guy have the gall to ask? It was like proposing on a first date. It was crazy. It was goddamn un-American.

"Is it always wrong to lie, Dad?" Jesse piped up.

What now?

"I dunno. Perhaps."

What was he getting at?

"Dad, I liked it when you were Father Christmas."

And the penny dropped. It was the book again, the King lying to his son. He was thinking of an answer when the car phone rang. He picked it up and grunted a yeah into it.

Jesse watched him, saw him lose color, saw him briefly lose control of the wheel, heard him say, "I can't believe it. . . . When? . . . Sure. . . . I'll try to get a flight this evening."

He replaced the phone. He looked, to Jesse, as if he had been hit by a baseball bat.

"What happened?" Jesse asked.

"It's Evan. He had an accident." The voice was a mere whisper.

"Is he dead?"

Dean nodded, then checked his mirror, and eased the car over to the curb and stopped, knuckled away a teardrop and got out.

Jesse watched him standing by the side of the road, gazing at nothing. He left his father alone for a few moments; then he grabbed his book, jumped out, went up to him, and tugged his sleeve.

"He'll come back," he said.

That decided, the little boy went back to the car and began reading his book. . . .

. . . *And they were the unconscious ones, the blessed young people, trapped by dreams and sated by the fulfillment of desire. The entire court of King Suddhodana slept in the palace gardens, their imaginations fueled and stimulated by wine and song, which had led to lovemaking beneath the stars. And now they slept, they and the dancers and the musicians who had entertained them, the only sound the sweet tinkling of a sitar until even that was silenced as the player fell into slumber.*

Nothing moved. The world was asleep. Peacocks nodded. Swans hid their heads. Birds nestled in the vines, and even the insects were motionless. The gods had put the world to sleep in order to achieve their purpose.

Only Siddhartha was awake. He crossed the gardens, whispering Channa's name. He stepped over a beautiful young woman, her eyes open, smiling at some pleasant dream. A tambourine tinkled as he stepped over another, knocking it from her arm, but still no one awoke.

At last he found Channa asleep on a step, entwined around the girl who had sung about the faraway lands. Siddhartha shook him, but Channa was reluctant to wake. He shook him again and whispered to him to get Kantaka, muffle his hooves, and come to the old gate; then he returned to the palace to say his last good-bye.

He climbed to the room on the roof of the world where he had been conceived and where his mother had died. Yasodhara lay asleep with her back to him, their newborn son in her arms. He came up to her to look into the baby's face, but as he reached the bed, she moved in her sleep and he could not see the child. And he knew that he was being tested by the gods— that if he wakened her and saw the little creature, then he would be tempted to stay, and he would remain a prisoner for the rest of his life. And so he turned away from them, and it was the first difficult decision he had had to make, the first unwilling act. He had had no training for self-denial.

When he reached the old gate, he found Channa waiting for him. He was holding Kantaka's reins, the stallion's hooves wrapped in straw and muslin.

Slowly they moved toward the gate past the sleeping guards. Only the great elephant was awake, and it curled its massive trunk in greeting, and as if in a dream—and as the gods had decreed—the gates opened, parting without a hand touching them, and Siddhartha walked out to discover the world. . . .

At daybreak they found themselves traveling through flat lands of savannah grass dotted with copses of thick vegetation, Kantaka cantering with both men on his back until they came to the edge of a wood that was known as Lumbini, and there Kantaka stopped without command.

Siddhartha dismounted and stared at the forest, not knowing where he was going. It was a journey without either map or plan. Slowly he walked forward. Channa, on Kantaka, called for him to come back, to remount for there were snakes and spiders and scorpions in the wood that could bite and sting through leather soles, but Siddhartha walked on, paying no heed.

It was Kantaka who first sensed the men. He whinnied a warning, and Siddhartha looked around him and saw creatures the like of whom he had never encountered, five of them, sitting beside a brook, naked and thin and filthy.

He turned to Channa and asked in a whisper who they were.

"Ascetics," Channa said.

"And why are they so thin, and naked?"

"They have given up all comforts of life, my lord. They have sworn never to leave the forest until they have reached Enlightenment."

Siddhartha smiled.

"Then they are looking for the same thing as I am," he said.

So saying, he took off his gold chain and unbuckled his sword, gathered his ringlets into a tail like that of Kantaka's, and with one hack of the sword cut away the locks that before had never seen a blade. And as he watched, Channa knew that his master had made a symbolic gesture and he wondered if this would be the last time he would see him, for men who renounced the world and cut off their hair were rarely seen again.

"Channa," Siddhartha said, "embrace my father and my wife and my child. Tell them that I shall not return until I have overcome death and rebirth."

Channa began to weep, and Siddhartha took his face in his hands and rubbed away the tears with his thumbs, then handed him his necklace and sword.

"These are for you," he said. "Channa, I am doing this for everyone. I am looking for freedom."

He stroked Kantaka's face as he had stroked Channa's; then he turned and walked toward the forest. He did not turn round, and Channa, watching, saw a beggar come out of the woods, holding a bowl and chanting the mantra of the lost souls.

Siddhartha walked toward him, and Channa at first could not believe what he was seeing, a proud prince of the Sakya race swapping clothes with a beggar. The last thing he saw of his master was a shorn man in rags disappearing into the forest and vanishing beneath a canopy of vines and branches, and it was the beggar who now walked erect, his humble posture transformed into haughty dignity.

Channa climbed onto Kantaka's back and tried to turn his head, but the stallion would not leave *until the last scent of his master had gone. Then he needed no further bidding. He galloped home and died when he reached the stable. . . .*

Siddhartha walked deep into the forest. A deer presented itself in front of him, unafraid; a parrot screeched a welcome from a shoulder-high branch; a python uncoiled itself and hung from a tree, its tongue flickering in front of Siddhartha's face as if attempting speech; an elephant made the noise of ten brass instruments; a rhinoceros scratched the ground and bowed its massive head. It was as if every living creature had turned out to welcome the newcomer.

He walked until he reached the bank of the river Anoma, where he stopped, sat beneath a tree, and closed his eyes.

Night fell. Siddhartha sat motionless until dawn, and when he woke, he saw the five Ascetics grouped in a semicircle in front of him. They were naked and filthy, hair and beards growing wild. The tongue of one flopped wolflike over his chin and hung almost to his collar bone. The hands of another had been clenched for so long that the nails had grown through the palms and out the back, and orchids had blossomed between each nail.

Siddhartha looked from one to the other, then at the sky. A monsoon cloud moved across the rising sun. Thunder crackled. A moment later the first raindrops spattered around them, and a giant cobra, the serpent-king Mucilinda, slithered toward them, past the five men, who stared at him in terror. Siddhartha closed his eyes once more and did not see Mucilinda approach, nor did he flinch when the snake began to coil himself around him. And as the torrent began, Mucilinda rose behind Siddhartha's neck and spread his mighty hood over him so that throughout the storm, which lasted all day, not a drop dampened him.

When it was over, Mucilinda uncoiled himself and departed, and when Siddhartha opened his eyes once more, the five men were lying prostrate before him in worship.

"My friends," Siddhartha said, "let us search for Enlightenment together and vow to be silent until we find it."

He touched both hands to his lips, and the Ascetics did the same.

$S_i x$

Dean had never indulged in introspection. He hadn't had the time. As for the great fundamental questions that Lisa had resurrected, well . . . the way he looked at it was that if the biggest brains on the planet hadn't come up with the answers, who was Dean Konrad to even consider them?

But he had had a week to think. Wondering about Evan had led inevitably to wondering about himself; a week of comparing and contrasting. He remembered an occasion not long ago when the subject of religion had come up and Evan had dismissed it. His religion was wheelin' an' dealin'. His office was his church, his phone was his rosary, and that night, with a bellyful of beer in him, Evan had boasted that he had gone out on the tightrope of life without any spiritual safety net.

Which was fine—until he slipped.

"Sir?"

He looked up; the flight attendant was looking at him with that anxious, professional grimace of a grin that meant "You okay, feller?" And he thought, maybe his lips had been moving; maybe, even worse, he had been talking aloud; verbalizing his anxieties, as the shrinks would have it.

"Can I get you anything?"

Yeah. Whiskey.

"You got it."

He looked across at Lisa, asleep in the window seat, and wondered how he was going to tell her. She wouldn't believe it. A week was a short time to do a mental U-turn, and if she asked why, he wouldn't be able to tell her because he wasn't sure himself.

Maybe it was the word *ashes* that was the catalyst. When the preacher had said the words over the open grave on that San Francisco hillside, Dean thought back to Jesse's comic book and the King washing his hands like Pontius Pilate.

"Ashes to ashes."

Looking into the grave as the clumps of earth clunked against the mahogany coffin, he thought about waste. Evan had left his mark sure enough, but what good had it done him? His God had been Mammon, and you couldn't pray to Mammon. And the hour with his mother at her house after the funeral had been terrible; this lonely little woman without a husband for five years and now without a son, her only child, and not even a daughter-in-law as a comfort. Her life was a vacuum now.

None of Evan's expensive women had turned up. Vultures only turned up when there was carrion to pick at. The last will and testament of a bankrupt was a paper mockery of a life.

On top of all that, the old woman would be haunted for the rest of her life by the possibility that Evan had committed suicide. She would go over and over the scene: a clear road, good visibility, and Evan was an excellent driver. The fact that the coroner had not come down on that particular side of the fence was little consolation. An open verdict was not much comfort.

Ashes to ashes.

Now he envied the Christians their faith in the afterlife, and especially he envied the Buddhists.

"He'll come back, Dad."

Jesse's words repeated in his brain like a hic-cup, like a looped cassette tape. Maybe if Evan had believed he'd be born again, he wouldn't have taken that corner so fast. Or maybe he would. Maybe he wanted another chance. Maybe he wanted to come back and start wheelin' an' dea-lin' all over again.

The whiskey came, and Dean cursed his way-ward imagination.

He glanced again at Lisa. She wasn't going to believe him. She'd just think he was running away. And she was probably right.

*   *   *

It was almost midnight by the time Lisa and Dean got home. Maria was full of condolences and offers of soup and sandwiches, but their cab was waiting for her and she went reluctantly.

They looked in on Jesse. He'd fallen asleep with the lights on and his book fallen on his chest. His new map of the Himalayas was tacked on the wall above the bed, and his jigsaw globe of the Earth was finished, except for the piece that was Tibet. He was holding it in his right hand, and when they tried to take it away, so that he wouldn't put it in his mouth, he gripped it tight and grumbled in his sleep, so they let him keep Tibet for the night.

Dean picked up the book, turned it over, and gazed at an illustration of a man sitting beneath a tree with a massive cobra coiled around him, its hood acting as an umbrella in a downpour. Five filthy characters sat naked around him. In the old days, just a week ago, Dean would have thought up a joke of a caption for it, but the week had diluted his sense of flippancy.

"My friends," Siddhartha said, "let us search for Enlightenment together and vow to be silent until we find it."

He read the sentence twice, took Jesse's bookmark from his bedside table, slipped it in, and laid the book down. Then he led Lisa out of the room and into their bedroom, took a deep breath and said it: "I think Jesse should go to Bhutan."

She whirled as fast as a dervish and the word *what* exploded from her like a violent sneeze.

"To Bhutan," he repeated as if he were suggesting a trip to the beach.

She wanted to know if he was joking.

He shook his head.

"It's just that I've changed my mind about a lot of things this past week."

He slumped into a chair and took off his shoes, knowing that the words sounded weak.

"But what are you saying?" Her hands were on her hips in the classic pose of the angry housewife. "Are you saying that you suddenly started to believe that Jesse is a Tibetan lama?"

"I thought you were the one who was open to the deal."

"Oh, come on." She whipped her head to one side in disbelief and frustration, and when she looked back at him, she was raging. "This is crazy. What's going on?"

He tried for levity, putting on the crooked grin that she always liked. "Nothing's going on. I just think it could be a good career opportunity for Jesse. . . ."

She glared at him.

"He'd get to wear all those little robes and sit on the floor and do meditation . . ."

But she wasn't buying.

"It's not funny," she said, deadly serious.

". . . hang out with other monks."

"It's not fucking funny."

Dean twitched, startled. Lisa didn't use that word. Ever. Not outside bed.

"Okay," he said. "It's just for a couple of weeks."

She still could not believe what he was saying,

but the anger had passed and now she was coldly rational.

"He can't go. He's got school. And I'm in the middle of my semester, so I can't take him."

And now he hit her with the second shot, following up the jab with a hook.

"I thought I could go with him."

And put her on the canvas.

"Just the two of you," she said in a whisper. "While I stay here?"

He could not look at her as she continued.

"But you've never looked after Jesse before. He's never been away from me."

She was pleading now, but he had to continue.

"There's nothing I can do here now," he said. "Except wait for lawyers to talk to lawyers, to talk to lawyers, to talk to lawyers. . . . Well then, great. Maybe it's the time I need to think about what to do with the rest of my life."

She began to cry. Silently, moisture oozing and beginning to drip.

"Without me?"

He got up and held her close.

"I love you, Lisa," he said, and couldn't remember when he had said it before and meant it, when he had last been protective—which was an irony, being protective when you were running away.

"You'd better," she said.

"It's just for a couple of weeks."

She pulled back and looked at him.

"But what happens if they decide Jesse is this reincarnation?" she said.

"They never will. They've already got another

candidate, remember? But if they ever did, well, then Jesse will decide for himself when he's older. Just as he will have to do with everything else in his life."

And Lisa gave in to the inevitable and just muttered Jesse's name over and over.

"You know," he said, "at the funeral I wished I did believe in reincarnation."

She pulled back again and smiled.

"You may have to. You may come back as the father of a spiritual god."

"Who? Me?"

"I'm sorry," she said, wiping away the tears. "I'm just upset. I'm upset with myself for not encouraging you, for not being with you and Jesse."

And then she hit him with a low blow.

"I'm upset with you for taking the adventure away from me."

Dean sighed. Added to the luggage he was checking through on this trip, she had just handed him a flight bag of guilt.

Part Two

Part Two

Seven

For what should have been a day and a night, the Air India jumbo had flown west, and time for Jesse was standing still. Every meal seemed to be a breakfast, yet he wasn't tired. His dad had tried to explain what jet lag was, but he was so excited that he chose not to believe in it. Jet lag had been filed under Fairy Stories, like Father Christmas and the legend of Siddhartha, except that he wanted to believe in Siddhartha.

The book was open on his lap, lit by the little light in the panel above his head. All the blinds were drawn, and the beam picked out the words:

. . . *And they were the unconscious ones . . . trapped by dreams.*

The only others awake were two flight attendants sitting by one of the doors. Jesse looked hard at them. They were beautiful with eyes as black as a moonless night and features of perfect symmetry, the younger one but a cobweb's breadth of the beauty of the other.

Jesse snapped the book shut and looked around. The airplane was silent except for the tinny tinkle of sitar music from the headset of a young man opposite, and then that died away as the tape came to an end. Now Jesse wanted someone to talk to. His father was asleep next to him in the window seat. Jesse fluttered his fingers in front of Dean's eyes but there was not even a flicker of an eyelash. An unconscious one trapped by dreams.

Jesse scrambled out into the aisle and up toward Chompa, who was stretched out across the three seats. Again Jesse tried his trick, and again he failed.

Farther back he saw Lama Norbu at a window seat, eyes closed, his head bowed. Jesse bounded into the empty seat in front of him and wiggled his fingers. The old man opened his eyes.

"Good morning, Jesse Long-Ears," he said.

Jesse smiled. "Are you praying?" he asked.

"I'm meditating."

"What is meditating?"

"It's a way to free the mind," the old man explained. "It's a way to detach yourself from the world, to watch your thoughts as if they were passing clouds . . . nothing more."

Jesse's smile broadened. "I love clouds," he said.

The Lama opened the blind and pointed out. Jesse leaned over the seat and saw the distant range of the Himalayas and the cumulus above.

"If we can learn to meditate in the right way," the Lama continued, "we can all reach Enlightenment."

"What's Enlightenment?"

"It's what we look for but we cannot describe."

Jesse was puzzled; this sounded like one of those "because" answers again. He was about to press the old man further, but the clouds drew his attention. They looked like a clump of trees, then became a whole white forest.

"Look," he whispered. "It's a tree. Lots of trees."

"Now look down," the Lama said. "That's where Siddhartha was born, and where he became the Buddha."

Jesse gazed down from thirty-five thousand feet, then turned and ran back. He had to get his book. He had to ask the Lama to read and explain. . . .

For six years Siddhartha and his followers lived in silence and never left the forest. For drink they had rain. For food they had a grain of rice or a broth of mud or small prey dropped by a passing bird. Nothing prepared by human hand fed them. They ate less than birds and drank less than frogs. They did not shelter from wind, rain, or sun, and they permitted snakes and mosquitoes to bite them.

Siddhartha became so thin that by pressing his stomach, he could feel his spine. Ivy grew round his feet and as far as his knees. He and the others were

107

trying to master suffering by denying their physical being; by making their minds so strong, they would forget about their bodies. And yet the knowledge that they were seeking was elusive . . . until one day Siddhartha received a message from the gods.

It was early morning, and he was wakened by the sound of a flute and a one-stringed instrument known as a vina. He opened his eyes and saw a herd of water buffaloes wallowing in front of him and a raft made of bamboo coming down the river. On it sat an old man and a boy. The old man was playing the flute, and the boy was plucking at the vina. They were playing the song of the faraway lands, which reminded Siddhartha of Yasodhara and a terrible melancholy blanketed him. Then, as they passed, he heard the old man tell the boy: "If you tighten the string too much, it will snap; and if you leave it too slack, it won't play."

The raft passed by. Neither the old man nor the boy saw Siddhartha because he had become the color of the tree trunk. He watched them until the raft disappeared around a bend, and when he could no longer hear the music, he started to get to his feet. It took him a long time, and it was painful. His bones creaked as he dragged his left foot from his thigh and tried to straighten his right leg. The ivy roots fought him and at first were stronger than he was. Every joint in his body crackled in protest. He took a deep breath that pained him as the air filled his deflated lungs. Slowly he got to his feet and leaned for a long time against the tree. Four of his followers were deep in meditation and did not see him, but the fifth, who stood on one leg by the riverbank, his hair reaching to his ankle, glared at him as he took his first step away from the tree.

He walked slowly, then turned and studied his footprints in the mud. No lotuses blossomed. Each tiny bone of his toes was clearly imprinted.

He hobbled to the riverbank and slithered into the water. The buffaloes stared at him but did not shy away. Small islands of lotus blossoms floated past him, some tickling him and making him shiver. He looked at his hands, and they seemed transparent; then he made cups of them and began to wash his face and his arms and his shoulders, bone against bone, with hardly any buffer of flesh, and as he washed, he thought he could feel himself crackle like a bunch of twigs ready for the fire.

When he had finished, standing waist deep in the river, he saw a young girl come toward him. Her name was Sujata. She was carrying a bowl of rice, and she stopped and offered it to him. At first Siddhartha thought that this was the work of Mara, the Evil One, tempting him, but the old man's words came back to him: "If you tighten the string too much, it will snap."

He took one grain of rice and ate, then offered the bowl back, but Sujata smiled at him and shook her head, and so he took more, and then a full handful. The man on one leg howled in rage and woke the others, and they came to the river's edge and stared silently at him. He raised the bowl and said, "Come and eat with me."

They shook their heads. A small bird flew out of the hair of one of them; then the one with the wolf's *tongue spat into the mud, and when he spoke, it was with the croak of a bullfrog.*

"You have betrayed your vows," he said. "You have abandoned the search."

Another said, "We can no longer follow you."

And another, "We can no longer learn from you."

Siddhartha knew now that he had been wrong. For twenty-nine years the string of the vina had been too slack, and for six years it had been too tight. Now he had to adjust it to play the tune. Neither self-indulgence nor self-mortification was the answer.

"To learn is to change," he told them. "The path to Enlightenment is the Middle Way. It is the line between all opposite extremes."

But they were not ready to understand. As one, they turned from him and wandered back into the forest. He watched them go and looked into the bowl. It was empty.

"If I can reach Enlightenment," he said to Sujata, "may this bowl float upstream."

He placed it in the river and watched as it slowly floated downstream, then stopped, spun twice, and began to move against the current.

And Siddhartha smiled.

First impressions were a disappointment. Dean had expected something alien. He'd seen the commercials and enough travelogues. At worst he expected squalor, at best something exotic, but Kathmandu Airport at night could have been Cincinnati. Clouds hid the Himalayas, and all he could see from the taxi on the way to the hotel was the occasional twinkling light.

Then they got out. They were in some sort of alley. Two monks were picking up the bags and motioning them to follow. Dean groaned loud enough for Chompa to ask what was wrong. He said, "Nothing." He couldn't be rude to his hosts. They were picking up the tab after all, but if he had known that he would be wandering up an alley watched by a couple of scrawny goats, alongside a stream trickling God knows what obscenities, then maybe he'd have thought twice . . . and the building he was being led to looked like something out of Auschwitz.

Reception was a table and a desk but no clerk and no formalities. The young monks led them along a narrow corridor, dotted with small blue doors, and Dean remembered that they called monks' room cells, didn't they? Plus he was jet-lagged.

Then the leading monk stopped and opened a door.

"This is your room," he said. "Very good room."

Dean looked in and saw a single naked light-bulb flickering uncertainly, two narrow iron beds with mattresses that looked like slabs out of a morgue. The lavatory was "en-suite," a cracked enamel bowl. There was a small window with shutters overlooking a courtyard.

"Welcome to Kathmandu," the monk said.

Automatically Dean went to his pocket and dragged out his billfold, but as he peeled off a note, the man turned and left, and Lama Norbu was saying good-night and hoping they slept well.

Dean glanced anxiously at Jesse to see how he was taking this idea of a Himalayan cell block, but he need not have worried. The boy ran to one of the beds and jumped on it, full of mischief.

Dean closed the door, pulled out a packet of cigarettes, and said to the wall, "I hope they allow smoking here."

"Don't worry, Dad," Jesse said. "I won't tell on you."

Dean looked at him, then stretched out in the bed, and lit up. Jesse got up and began to prowl the room like a puppy in a strange place.

"What is it?" Dean said. "I can't believe you're not tired."

"Dad, I know that smell," he said, his nostrils twitching.

"It's incense. Like they had at the Dharma Center. Nothing from your previous life. They burn it all the time."

He got up and began to unpack, wondering what they did for cupboards here. He hadn't expected a jacuzzi or a mini-bar, but maybe a wire coat hanger. . . .

"Hey, Dad," Jesse said. "Lama Norbu told me a story about a crane and a bunch of crayfish."

"Oh, yeah?"

"A crane like a bird, not a crane like in a construction site."

"Sure."

"Anyway . . ."

The story seemed to go on forever, all about two pools in a forest, one almost dried up, the other deep and covered in lotus blossoms. The fish were stuck in the small pool and close to death. Then the crane passed by and offered to take the fish, one by one, in its bill to the deep pool.

One of the fish was a cynic. He didn't believe the bird, and so, as a trial run, the crane offered to take one fish, let him see the pool, swim around for a bit . . .

Dean yawned.

. . . then come back and tell the others.

"Well," Jesse continued. "This is what happened, and the fish were convinced, so the crane took the same fish back, but this time he ate it and left the bones on the ground. And he did this with every one until the last one, the sin . . . sin . . ."

"Cynical," Dean said.

"Yeah, the cynical one was left, but he said, 'Don't carry me in your bill, O Crane. I'll ride on your back.' And so he did and saw the bones of his friends and realized what had happened. He waited until he was almost at the pool, then tightened his claws round the crane's neck until it broke, then he dropped off into the pool."

Jesse grinned and jumped up and down on the bed. "So. What does the story tell us?"

"Don't trust fish."

"No, Dad. Don't be dumb, Dad. It teaches us that wickedness does not always win and that every crane will meet its crayfish."

"Yeah, right," Dean said and yawned deeper.

"What's wrong, Dad?"

He turned. The boy was looking at him like a concerned parent anxious about a child.

"Nothing, Jesse," Dean said wearily. "But we've been traveling for over twenty hours, so shut your eyes and just pretend you're asleep. Maybe you'll get lucky."

No chance. A pause, then another "Da—aad."

Dean's patience snapped. "For God's sake," he yelled, "go to sleep,"

The boy twisted away from him, pulled the pillow over his head, and curled into the fetal position. Dean wanted to go over and say he was sorry for yelling, sorry for taking Jesse away from his mother and his school. But the rage was still boiling in him, and so he went out. At the door he turned.

"I'm going to take a walk and I want you to be asleep when I get back."

The pillow jerked twice, Jesse beneath it, nodding in obedience.

Now he could add guilt to his apprehension. Cursing beneath his breath he wandered along the fetid corridor, stropping briefly at each door, listening to the snoring. At the end he turned a corner and came to a large door. He pushed it open. It creaked as it swung back, and he gazed into the massive stone face of the Buddha.

The statue dominated the room. Dean figured it as maybe twenty feet from the top of the head to the crossed legs and lit only by fluttering butter lamps so that, with the breeze from the open window, shadows flickered across the face. Large, intricate poster-color paintings covered the walls, but it was the eyes of the Buddha that attracted Dean's eyes as if by magnetism.

A monk sat cross-legged in the far corner, intoning a mantra: *"Om mani padone hum."*

Over and over.

Dean gazed at him and inhaled the incense.

"Om mani padone hum."

Again and again, the mantra becoming, in Dean's brain, the sound of a swarm of bees. He shivered. Sweat broke out on his forehead and upper lip. His memory dredged up terrible sermons of his Presbyterian childhood, of the price of sin being an eternity of hellfire, and the awful panic when he was six and burnt his finger on a match and could not comprehend the notion of an eternity of that scorching pain. . . .

"Don't be afraid, Dad."

He felt Jesse's hand squirm into his and looked down at the boy's face, and the poet's words came back to him: "The child is father of the Man."

Afraid? Too strong a word, wasn't it? Here he was, a hundred and eighty pounds of U.S. male with a sixteen-five college boxing record, almost good enough for the Golden Gloves.

Afraid?

No. Surely not. Just spooked a bit. That's all.

He grinned at Jesse and picked him up. As he turned to go, he could have sworn that the smiling stone Buddha winked at him.

Kathmandu.

Geography had never been one of Dean's strongest subjects. Kathmandu was one of those places you could spell three or four ways. There was something about a little green-eyed idol to the north of it, wasn't there? The town where old hippies went to die.

If he had considered it at all in his subconscious, he would have expected filth and despair, poverty and sly villains out of *Indiana Jones* tugging at his sleeve.

What he saw was bustle and color, a swirl of perpetual motion, of seemingly happy-go-lucky chaos. The insults traded between drivers, the cyclists and motorized rickshaw bikes seemed haphazard and even affectionate. A cow chewed its cud in the middle of the street. And at last, there, in all their magnificence, were the Himalayas.

They were riding in a cramped three-wheel taxi, he, Jesse, Lama Norbu, and Chompa, and it was the young monk who was acting as guide and translator, pointing out the peaks of the mountain range, telling him where Everest was in relation to Annapurna, telling him that the little taxi was called a *pudrej*, that the chant he had heard last night was roughly translated as "Hail to the jewel in the lotus," and was the invocation of the bodhisattva of infinite compassion who was called Avalokitesnavara.

"Huh?" Dean said.

"Ava-lock-it—"

Then Chompa was interrupted by a shout, and the taxi stopped, and they saw another young monk waving at them.

"This is Sangay," Chompa said. "He will lead us to candidate number two."

They piled out, and there was much bowing. Then Sangay said, "His name is Raju. He comes from a very poor family."

Lama Norbu nodded. "Yes, I read the report," he said. "The dreams are the interesting part. They are remarkably similar."

"Almost identical. Fifteen different monks. The same dream. A little circus."

"I know, but I haven't seen his charts yet."

"They are perfect," Sangay said. "Like Jesse's. Classic astrology. But it is what you feel when you see him that matters most."

Again the old man nodded. First a young blond American; now a circus boy. It was typical of Lama Dorje, always joking, always setting little tests, and Lama Norbu remembered the words from Kempo Tenzin's dream: "I have always found life amusing and see no need to change now."

Always a joker, but this was on the grandest scale of all, to send them halfway around the world and then bring them back to find his *tulku* virtually on their doorstep. Some joke.

In front of them Jesse and Dean, hand in hand, turned out of the street into a square and stopped in their tracks. The building that confronted them was the most awesome Dean had ever seen. His camera seemed to come alive in his hand, so eager was he to get a record of it, just in case this was some sort of optical illusion, some mirage brought on by jet lag.

The backdrop was a plaza of crooked medieval houses, with turrets, attics, and balconies, leaning Pisa-like in all directions and painted in a variety of colors, built, it seemed at first, haphazardly; but as he gazed around, Dean felt that perhaps it was by design, as if the turret on the western side complemented the attic opposite.

Then there was the building itself. Automatically he made calculations. A pure white construction, the building was fifty yards square, the base maybe ten feet high, then rising in a series of stepped levels to a white hemisphere topped with a cube. The cube was twenty feet square with an eye painted in startling colors on each side, gazing at the points of the compass, and the whole thing was capped by a tiered pyramid painted in gold.

Jesse whistled and whispered, "Isn't it great?"

"Yeah. It's looking at us."

"It's a dome, like on your building."

Dean grinned and ruffled his hair. "D'you think they copied me?"

"Good joke, Dad," Jesse said. Then they turned as Lama Norbu came across to them.

"This is the Bodanath Stupa Square," he said. "The *stupas* were originally burial mounds, but now they are monuments. This is one of the most sacred in Asia. The square base is the symbol of the earth. The dome is the symbol of water. The eyes are the levels of Enlightenment or fire. The umbrella is the symbol of air. And right at the top is the symbol of the sun and the moon together, the unity of opposites."

So astonished was he at the sight that it took Dean a moment to notice the crowd. It was like a massive, colorful fancy dress party. It was Mardi Gras and the Rio Carnival, a fusion of primary colors, even the poorest in threadbare robes were colorful with their jewelry of coral and turquoise bracelets and necklaces. A group of monks in maroon filed past them, twirling prayer wheels that were set into the wall of the *stupa*.

"Tibetans like me," Lama Norbu said. "Some of them have walked for days to get here. Then they will go back, try to avoid the Chinese patrols."

Dean looked at the old man for signs of bitterness, but there was not a trace of anger in his face. On the flight he had read about the atrocities, about nuns and monks being forced to copulate in front of the people of Lhasa, of the mummified remains of the Lamas being fed to dogs, so that now every body was automatically cremated to avoid this ultimate humiliation. A whole nation had turned the other cheek.

"Lama, Lama . . ." Jesse's voice punctured Dean's thoughts. He looked down to see the boy pulling at the old man's sleeve, with one hand and pointing at the prayer wheels with the other. "Can I go round and touch these things?"

"Of course," he said. "And remember, you should always walk clockwise."

Jesse looked up at Dean for approval.

"He'll be quite safe," the old man said, and Dean thought: Yeah, safe enough here among these people, safer than most places back home maybe, and anyway Dean was planning to go up on the *stupa* and he could keep an eye on Jesse. The boy would be easy enough to spot, the only blond head in a baseball cap in the place.

A rendezvous was arranged at a coffee shop nearby, and they went off, hand in hand to the wall, then Dean climbed a set of steps, gave Jesse the thumbs-up, and watched him go, walking quickly along, copying the others, twirling the prayer wheels, making them clack. Then Dean turned, gazed at the *stupa*, and pulled a notebook from his back pocket.

Jesse's mind was a cauldron of excitement. This was great. This was really, really foreign, and he thought of the guys back home. He checked his watch. They'd be doing Geography right now, and I'm doing it for real. Then he remembered the time difference. They'd be *asleep* right now, and he chuckled at the idea.

A gang of kids in robes jostled him and twisted his cap round back to front, but he didn't feel any animosity toward them. It wasn't like at home when the big kids came along and poked and prodded you till you lashed out; these kids were okay. They were chattering at him in their funny language, and he shrugged and held up his hands in mock surrender, they just laughed and ran off.

He got to the end of the wall, turned, and nearly fell over an old man who was sitting with his back to the wall, cross-legged. He was naked except for a loincloth, and covered with ash. Jesse took a step back and stared at him, but the old man did not acknowledge him. He looked closer, but the man just seemed to look through him, and Jesse imagined that maybe if he touched the man's stomach, he would feel right through to his backbone.

He walked on past him, keeping tight to the wall, clacking the wheels. Then, as if someone was pulling him by wires, he wandered off into the crowd toward the sound of brash music and the clash of a tambourine and, through the crowd, saw three boys and a girl, all around his age. They were ragged and half naked. Two of the boys were dancing to the tinny sound of an ancient record player. The girl was playing a tambourine. A monkey in a hat and red waistcoat was jiggling a tin cup. But it was the third boy who fascinated Jesse—a barefooted urchin in a torn shirt, juggling with four balls that seemed to be on fire, flames spurting from them. But the boy wasn't burned; he just leaped around as if plugged into an electrical socket, all the while grinning like a maniac.

Then Jesse twitched and took a nervous step back as the monkey leaped from the girl's shoulder and ran up to him, rattling its can. It looked at him, head on one side and then went to the next onlooker, who dropped in a coin, and the monkey bowed.

Jesse was so mesmerized by the little urchin's performance that he did not see Lama Norbu and Sangay approach and gaze at the two of them.

"That's the other boy isn't it?" the Lama whispered.

"Yes, that's Raju."

"They have found each other," the Lama said and shook his head in astonishment. It was Lama Dorje again, he thought, up to his tricks.

They watched as the little boy came up to Jesse. They stared in silence at each other for a moment. Then Raju spoke in English, a gruff voice, deep and confident.

"Hey, you wanna see more tricks?"

Jesse nodded and grinned. The kid had an American accent.

"How much you give? Ten rupees?"

Jesse shrugged.

"Five rupees?"

Jesse shook his head.

"One rupee?"

"I don't have any money."

Raju pointed. "What's in your pocket?"

"It's my Gameboy." He pulled it out and offered it. "You wanna try?"

Why not? Jesse thought. Kathmandu versus Seattle, and there could be only one winner.

Raju's face set in a frown of concentration, and his thumbs became a blur. The group closed in to watch, and the monkey jumped onto Raju's shoulder.

Jesse blinked. The kid was brilliant.

"You're good," he said.

"Oh yeah, thanks," Raju said, deep in concentration. "I'm the champion of Kathmandu."

It was going to be a big win for Nepal, and Jesse was wondering how he was going to save face here, when the monkey intervened, grabbed the Gameboy, and scuttled off, followed immediately by the four kids, all yelling its name. "Tashi, Tashi. . . ."

Briefly Jesse stood motionless in shock; then he ran after them, furious that he'd let himself be conned. Only five minutes in the Third World and some midget who didn't reach to his shoulder had swindled him out of fifty bucks of computer game.

He ran across the square and saw the monkey scamper down an alley, followed by the urchin. It seemed as if the crowd was on their side because he had to push and jostle his way through, and by the time he had reached the turning, he had lost them.

The alley was narrow. A stream ran down the center of it. A crowd was haggling in front of a stall. Jesse could not get through, and so he crawled between sandals; then, as he got to his feet, he looked into the eyes of three goats. They had been beheaded and skinned except for wispy beards which fluttered in the breeze. Jesse shivered and ran on to the end of the alley, which gave onto a square. He looked left and right, but there was no sign of the monkey.

Slowly he trudged across the square. People went about their business and paid him no heed. Men forked bales of straw onto carts. A potter worked at his wheel. Others stood on grinding wheels, whipping them into frenzied motion.

Jesse sat on a step and looked back the way he had come. There were so many identical alleys leading off the square, he couldn't remember which one he had run along in his haste to find the goddamn monkey. He was lost, and he was in danger of bursting into tears, but, he thought, To hell with that, I'm an American, I'm not gonna let these medieval people see me cry. He'd just have to pull himself together, that's all. When the going gets tough, and all that. . . . Then a voice behind him made him jump.

"Hey!"

He turned. The urchin was standing on the step above, holding out the Gameboy, the monkey on his shoulder.

"Tashi is a very bad monkey," he said, and swiped it with his free hand. "But also very clever."

And suddenly everything was okay again.

Dean had lost track of time. He had half filled his notebook with sketches and had taken three rolls of film. He was amazed at and humbled by the mind that had designed the monument. He had checked its lines against the compass mark on the street map and saw that the *stupa* had been built exactly north to south; it was perfect symmetry, each of the four eyes gazing out at the four points of the compass. It was geometric poetry.

As he looked at the map, he caught sight of his watch and felt guilty that for the past forty minutes he hadn't thought of Jesse, and now he scanned the crowds and couldn't see him. By the time he got to the coffee shop, he was becoming anxious, and by his second cup his anxiety was solidifying into fear. Soon, if Jesse did not show, he would begin to panic.

He glanced across the room to where Lama Norbu sat. Somehow his reactions to events were important indicators. He was a leader. Watching him, Dean felt as he did when there was bad turbulence in flight. You watched the flight attendants. If they didn't look worried, then the wings weren't about to drop off; and so, if the old man was unconcerned, there was nothing to worry about. He saw him reach into his robe, produce a small box, and take a black pill.

Chompa sat at the next table, idly gazing out over the square, and Dean leaned over and asked softly, "Is Lama Norbu ill?"

Chompa took his time answering. "He is not completely well," he said, "but very strong."

Then Dean saw Jesse at the door. He was leading a ragged, barefoot urchin into the shop. Three others stood by the window, pressing their noses against the glass.

"Dad, Dad," he shouted, "this is my new friend. I got lost and he found me and—"

Lama Norbu interrupted by getting to his feet and holding up a hand for silence. "We know, Jesse, we know," he said. "We have been waiting for you both."

Then he placed his palms together and bowed low in front of the urchin. "I am very pleased to meet you, Raju," he said as he straightened up. "Sangay has told me much about you. It is good that two of the candidates have found each other in this way. It is just like one of Lama Dorje's jokes."

The boys were still holding hands. Now they

turned and stared at one another, and each took a step backward. Identical expressions, a mirror image of astonishment—but it was the Lama's phrasing that confused Dean.

"Two of the candidates?"

Not, "You two candidates."

The question was immediately answered. Lama Norbu took an envelope from the folds of his robes and laid it on the table.

"And now we must visit a third," he said with a trace of weariness, "whom I have only just heard of. It will be a very long drive, so let us hope that it will be Lama Dorje's last joke."

A van was hired, and Dean offered to drive. The Tibetans did not seem too keen and it would gave him something to do, a chance to take charge a little, to be something other than a chaperon. It was a wreck with a gearshift and he'd driven an automatic for years, but he soon got the hang of it. Kathmandu was chaos anyway, and he happily bumped along with Chompa next to him. When he cut off a *pudrej*, Chompa grinned at him.

"When in Rome, do like Romans," he said, and Dean wondered where he had come across the saying.

When they were out on the open road, heading southeast, Dean asked about the letter, and Chompa told him. It had been sent to the monastery and redirected to the hostel.

Dean glanced in his mirror at the two boys, the latest monk, the Lama, and the monkey. He began to wonder if he was going to turn into some

Flying Dutchman here, forever traveling around Asia, having to hire bigger and better vans as they filled up with eight-year-olds. Then, at a word from Lama Norbu, he turned south onto a dirt track.

He drove for an hour across dusty plains dotted with clumps of savannah grass; the only other traffic was the occasional bullock cart.

Maybe it was the air, but he felt light-headed as if he had smoked some dope. Or maybe it was the presence of the Lama and the two monks, but he felt kind of spiritual. Or maybe it was just the combination of lingering jet lag and culture shock, but he was beginning to feel seduced by the place.

"What is it, Dad?" Jesse wanted to know, as if he were reading Dean's mind.

"I think I'm turning into a hippie," he said.

"Well," Jesse said, grinning at him. "Keep it to yourself."

He grinned back into the mirror. Raju winked at him and held up his hand, flashing his fingers at him. The Gameboy series was getting desperate. Nepal was ahead by twenty-two to fifteen.

Again he lost track of time. Now and again he looked over his shoulder, hoping to catch sight of Everest, but the mountains were lost in a heat haze, and the horizon was a shimmering illusion. Then the Lama nudged him, pointed toward a clump of trees, and Dean swung the wheel.

The track led through trees and up to a crumbling mansion that must once have been grand, a place of pillars, wide verandahs and cornices, and

Dean had visions of the old days, of iced tea served beneath ceiling fans pulled by punkah wallahs and orders lazily given in drawling English accents, a Merchant-Ivory sort of a place, now gone to seed.

The stone steps leading to the mahogany door had crumbled. The gardens had been unattended for years, and there was a smell of rotting vegetation and unwanted compost.

As Dean braked, a side door opened and an old woman came slowly down the stairs. She was carrying a *kata* and waited until Lama Norbu had eased himself out of the van, then greeted him with a smile.

"Dharma gossip has arrived before you," she said. "Is it true that one of the other candidates is American?"

"Yes, Ani-La," he said, indicating Jesse. "Lama Dorje was always surprising."

The old woman walked across to Jesse, touched his hair, and shook her head and smiled.

Then she turned as a middle-aged woman in an elegant sari came down the steps. She bowed low in front of Lama Norbu, then stood up and said that she hoped the journey had not been too tiring.

"No," he said. "And now I want to meet the other child."

The woman turned. Standing on the verandah was a young girl in a red sari. She was tall and elegant and serious.

Jesse and Raju glanced at her curiously, then looked past her into the house.

"Here is my precious one," the woman said.

The boys stared at each other, then back at the girl, who was walking forward and being introduced by her mother to the Lama. Silently she went through the *kata* ritual with him, then turned and walked up to the boys, throwing her head back in disdain.

"I am the real Lama Dorje," she said, head erect. "And you are both fakes."

Jesse blinked. Raju shook his head at the challenge.

"Lama Dorje wasn't a woman," Raju said.

"He was," she said defiantly, and looked Raju up and down as if he had just crawled out of a sewer. "She was the abbess of a convent. But how could you know? You don't even go to school." Then she turned on Jesse. "And you're just a foreigner."

Jesse blinked again. Just a foreigner indeed. He was about to say he wasn't a foreigner, he was an American. It was she who was just a foreigner. Everybody knew that Americans weren't foreign, but she was not about to let him interrupt. She posed dramatically, hands on hips, and said, "I have a secret garden."

Then she spread her arms like a ballet dancer, spun on one heel, and marched off toward a thick grove of trees, calling over her shoulder: "Come. Come, ignorant boys."

Jesse and Raju turned to Lama Norbu, who smiled at them and nodded his agreement; then they were off, chasing after her, Tashi scampering at their heels.

Lama Norbu turned to the others. "She is quite right, you know," he said. "Five lives ago Lama Dorje was a very famous woman, the head of an important convent in Tibet."

He made the introductions. Ani-La was a nun from a convent thirty miles away. Gita's mother was named Sonali, and once they were seated on the verandah, she told her story.

"My late husband came from Tibet," she said. "He was a man of great faith, and he knew Lama Dorje. Every year he made a donation to his monastery. Then one day the Lama came here unannounced, just appeared at the door like a miracle. It was the year before he died. He stayed for two days, and just as he was leaving, he placed his hand on my stomach. I did not know what it meant, this gesture, but immediately after he died, I became pregnant, something I had thought was impossible."

She smiled at the memory, and the nun took up the story.

"A month ago she wrote to me to come right away because a most amazing thing had happened. One night the child—"

Sonali interrupted, anxious to tell the tale. "Gita was chanting prayers in Tibetan, saying things I couldn't understand."

"She was speaking the lotus mantra," Ani-La said. "How could she know that?"

She looked from one face to another, searching for an answer.

It was simple, Dean thought. Lama Dorje knew the lotus mantra. Lama Dorje was Tibetan.

Q.E.D.

All you needed to work it out was a belief in reincarnation.

Gita's secret garden was walled on all sides and overgrown with grass and vines. Two six-foot stone cobras reared out of cracked and empty water tanks. Their tongues protruded, their hoods were spread. Jesse, as he passed one, reached out toward the tongue, then jerked back in case it suddenly came alive and spat venom at him. He wasn't taking any chances in this strange country. From a safe distance he stared into the jeweled eyes, trying to hypnotize it as he had seen a mongoose do on TV back home; then he turned as Gita tapped his shoulder. She was posing again, looking first at him, then at Raju.

"So, pretenders," she said. "It is too bad you had to come all this way for nothing."

The boys glanced at each other and began to circle her, united by her attack. Then they stopped on either side of her.

Raju pointed to Jesse. "He is Lama Dorje," he said.

"No," Jesse said. "Raju is Lama Dorje."

Gita shook her head, twirled away from them, and confronted them again, hands on hips.

"Right here in this garden," she said, "my grandfather, who was a rajah and a great saint, was eaten by a tiger." Dramatically she pointed to the spot in the corner beneath a tree.

Jesse looked at her in astonishment, Raju with suspicion.

"There was a terrible famine," she said. "The tiger was looking for food to feed her babies, and so my grandfather offered himself."

Jesse pretended to spit. "Must have been pretty stupid," he said.

Gita looked at him scornfully. "Only a great being could do something like that," she said.

Jesse was impressed, but he couldn't show it, not in the face of such disdain, and so he mocked her by turning to Raju.

"Eat me, you poor, hungry tiger," he said.

Raju growled, dropped onto all fours, and darted at him, cuffing his knee and spitting. Then they were off, running round the garden until Gita stopped them by holding out a necklace. Hanging from it was a yellow tooth. She swung it as if trying to hypnotize them.

"This," she said, "belonged to the tiger that ate my grandfather."

Again Jesse, despite himself, was impressed. He took it from her and studied it and did not hear Raju whisper to the girl, "You can't fool me. I've heard that story a thousand times. But he doesn't know that."

Jesse held the tooth up. "Your grandfather must have been pretty tough if the tiger lost this on him."

For a moment there was a standoff, and Jesse wondered how she would take it, as a joke or an insult; then she smiled and took the necklace back.

"As holder of the Tiger's Tooth," she announced,

"I make you both members of the secret society of King Cobra."

A truce had been called, but Gita hadn't seen Tashi. He leaped at her from the undergrowth, snatched the tooth, and scampered off and over the garden wall, the children whooping in pursuit.

Jesse was the quickest. He flung himself at Tashi, but the monkey dodged him and leaped for the hanging branch of a tree. Jesse stopped and looked up. He had never seen such a tree. The main trunk, he reckoned, must be six feet in diameter. His dad had taught him how to calculate in his head. Then he counted. Twelve subsidiary trunks branched out from the main one, forming a canopy about twenty feet square. The knots in the exposed roots were as big as footballs. Tashi screeched at him and dangled the bracelet tantalizingly out of reach. Then Jesse turned to see the others coming along the path with the adults, Gita in the lead, acting as guide.

"Did you know that Siddhartha reached Enlightenment under this tree?" she said to Raju. Then she smiled up at Lama Norbu. "Well, a tree just like this one."

Jesse looked at the old man. "Is it true?" he asked.

The old man smiled. "It must have been very like this tree," he said. The Lama looked up at Tashi, reached out, and beckoned. The monkey dropped the necklace into his hand, and the old man put it round Gita's neck, then sat beneath the tree, and the children squatted in a semicircle around him.

It was outside a village called Bodgaya. Siddhartha made his way toward the great tree and saw Svastika the reaper working at the side of the road. He asked him for some grass so that he might have some protection from the hard ground during the length of his meditation. Svastika cut him eight handfuls, which Siddhartha scattered around the trunk, and the cuttings formed themselves into a chair. Siddhartha bowed seven times, then sat cross-legged with his back to the tree and vowed not to move until he had achieved supreme knowledge, even if his skin were to parch or his bones crumble to dust.

No sooner had he closed his eyes than Mara, the Evil One, sensed danger, knowing that if Siddhartha were to find peace and impart the knowledge, Mara's grip over humanity would be loosened. And so Mara sent his five daughters to tempt him. They were the spirits of Pride, Greed, Fear, Ignorance, and Desire. Each one could ruin a man. All five together would be irresistible.

They approached him in the guise of village girls, graceful figures dressed in red and gold saris. One carried a sitar, another a tambourine, another an earthenware jar, and they knew that Siddhartha was aware of them even with his eyes closed for they had bathed in scented water and smelled like young girls in summer.

The seduction began. The first walked past Siddhartha to the well that bubbled through the roots of the tree. She drew water and filled the jar, then lowered her sari to her waist and washed her body. A second sat opposite him, mimicking his cross-legged posture, then loosened her hair and began combing it, gazing into his face without blinking, but he did not open his eyes.

The third and fourth sat by the well and played the sitar and the tambourine, and the rhythm caused the others to sway and dance before him. Finally the fifth, the spirit of Desire, stretched out in front of him within touching distance and caressed the neck of the jar as if caressing a lover, and still Siddhartha did not open his eyes, not even when she tipped it over and the water gushed out to form a pool in front of him.

Mara knew that his daughters had failed him. He had disguised the temptations in the simplest forms, but Siddhartha was looking beyond form, beyond the present.

Mara was enraged and entered the arena, and the force of his rage pried open Siddhartha's eyelids. He gazed into his reflection in the pool that lapped at his feet and saw Mara's hideous face and knew that the battle was truly joined.

Mara exploded out of the water like a spouting whale, his toothless mouth screaming, his red eyes rimmed with mucus. The sky went black, and a poisonous wind howled in harmony. The force of the gale made his daughters wince and huddle together for protection, but there was no escape from his rage. They had failed him, and the wind covered them with shrouds of leaves and turned

*them to dust and scattered them to the four corners
of the earth.*

*Now Mara brought the elements into play. He
controlled lightning, storm, and thunder. Fireballs
were at his command. He ordered the malign forces
of Nature to attack Siddhartha. But as the storm
began to build, Siddhartha took strength from the
power of the intellect and shielded himself with the
armor of meditation.*

*"What is the cause of old age and death?" he
asked himself.*

"The answer is birth.

"What is the cause of existence?

"The answer is ties."

The elements attacked him.

"There are ties because there is desire.

"There is desire because there is sensation."

*Lightning flickered around the tree like the
tongue of Mucilinda the Serpent King and started
small fires, but Siddhartha was unharmed. Fireballs became candlelight as they reached the tree
and then turned into fireflies and glowworms.*

*"What is the cause of sensation?" Siddhartha
asked himself.*

"The answer is contact."

Then he began to chant:

"Om mani padone hum. . . ."

*Over and over until the sound was like that of a
million humming birds, and Mara went crazy. He
covered his ears, but still the mantra leaked into his
poisoned brain, and he begged Siddhartha to stop,
and in his compassion Siddhartha fell silent.*

The wind died down and the world was still. It was as if the earth were holding its breath.

Mara took his hands from his ears and glared at Siddhartha, and he could read the mind of the man in deepest meditation.

"What is the cause of contact?

"The answer is the six senses.

"What is the cause of the six senses?

"The answer is name and form

"What is the cause of name and form?

"The answer is perception.

"What is the cause of perception?

"The answer is impression.

"What is the cause of impression?

"The answer is ignorance."

And Mara roared in frustration and called up his army.

Again the night was black. Low clouds blocked out the moon and the stars. On the horizon a terrible force appeared: a thousand men in serried ranks, armored and helmeted in black metal, quilled and bristling with spears and pikes and instruments of torture and death.

Such was Mara's power that again Siddhartha was forced to open his eyes and to gaze into ultimate terror. He tried to look for help and compassion in the faces of Mara's army, but behind the grilled helmets he saw only skulls, rictus grins, and eyeless sockets. He knew that there was no pity to be found, and so he turned back on himself, reversing the process of his meditation.

"Ignorance is the root of suffering," he told himself.

"Suppress ignorance by suppressing impression.

"Suppress impression by suppressing perception.

"Suppress perception by suppressing name and form."

As one, each skeletal soldier drew an arrow from his quiver. The head of each arrow was smeared with pitch. From left and right, crippled dwarfs carrying torches hobbled along the lines, setting the arrows alight, and when every arrow was lit, the bows were drawn, and the clouds were spiked by red streaks.

Drums began to beat.

"Suppress name and form by suppressing the six senses," Siddhartha told himself.

The bows were drawn taut now, the army a motionless tableau except for the blurred forearms of the drummers.

"Suppress the six senses by suppressing contact.

"Suppress contact by suppressing sensation.

"Suppress sensation by suppressing desire."

Mara screamed, the archers loosed their arrows, and they hissed skyward like angry birds and disappeared into the clouds.

"Suppress desire by suppressing ties.

"Suppress ties by suppressing existence."

Silence as the arrows reached their apex and dropped, became red tips spearing the clouds as they hurtled toward Siddhartha.

"Suppress existence by suppressing birth.

"Suppress birth by suppressing old age and death."

The arrows converged as if by some magnetic

force, and Siddhartha opened his eyes and welcomed them.

"To exist is to suffer.

"Desire leads to rebirth.

"By stifling desire we prevent birth.

"And prevent suffering.

"Holiness stifles desire, and we cease to endure birth and suffering."

And the arrows turned to lotus petals and floated gently toward him, landing in his hair, in his lap, and filling his cupped hands.

The clouds dispersed and the army was no more. A full moon rose and cast its light upon the tree and the pool. A cricket chirped.

Lotus petals dissolved on the surface of the pool as Siddhartha gazed at his reflection. For a moment he sat motionless, then reached forward with his right hand and touched the water. His reflected fingers curled around his wrist, and he pulled his reflection out from beneath the pool to face him.

And the reflection spoke: "You who will go where no one else will dare, will you be my God?"

"It is hard to be born so many times," Siddhartha said. "Architect, finally I have met you. You will not rebuild your house again."

"But I am your house, and you live in me," his reflection said.

Siddhartha touched the ground with his left hand and said, "O Lord of my own ego, you are pure illusion. You do not exist. The earth is my witness."

And his reflection metamorphosed into the bloated body and hideous face of Mara, but there was no longer any terror in him, only the resigned *look of the defeated. Then the vision vanished, leaving Siddhartha alone, cocooned in compassion.*

Lama Norbu looked from one child to the other. "Siddhartha alone won the battle against an army of demons through the force of his love and the great compassion he had found, and he achieved the great calm that precedes detachment from emotions.

"He had reached beyond himself. He was beyond joy or pain, separate from judgment, able to remember that he had been a girl, a dolphin, a tree"—he glanced at Tashi—"a monkey. He remembered his first birth and the millions after that. He could see beyond the universe.

"He had seen the ultimate reality of all things. He had understood that nothing happens by chance, that every movement in the universe is an effect provoked by a cause. He knew there was no salvation without compassion for every other being. From that moment on, Siddhartha was called the Buddha, the awakened one."

Jesse raised his hand, and Chompa smiled, reminded of the smallest of the boy monks.

"What did he mean about the Architect?" he asked.

Lama Norbu chuckled. "He wasn't talking about your father. He meant the prison of oneself. And that"—he tapped his temple—"is as much as this old man can tell you."

Eight

Nothing that Dean had anticipated had prepared him for the flight in the mountains. It was a small, single-engined aircraft with the words *Royal Bhutan* on the fuselage in maroon. When the pilot invited him into the cockpit, he could not believe the altimeter. It read fourteen thousand feet, and yet, when Dean glanced back along the aisle—at the Lama, the two monks, the nun and the three children—he saw that everyone was looking up at the mountains—even Tashi. Surely no one lived at this height.

"Oh, yes," the pilot said. "In Bhutan people live at sixteen thousand feet."

"Don't they need oxygen?"

"Oh, no. Plenty oxygen. Good air." The pilot

smiled. "I've been to Los Angeles. Not much oxygen there. And now you'd better go back to your seat and fasten your belt. We are coming in to land."

On the way back, Dean looked out.

Land? Land where? All he could see was mountain.

He sat down, buckled up, and stared at a rock face; he turned round and looked at Jesse two seats behind. The boy gave him the thumbs-up, and when he turned round again, a hairline gap had opened up in the Himalayas. There was a lurch and a drop, and they were through the gap and heading down to a green valley and a hut with a wind sock outside.

The runway was a strip of grass. Customs and Immigration was a man in a robe in his hut. Then they were off, in a bullock cart, heading north into the hills, an American and his son, two monks, a Lama, a nun, two Nepalese children, and a monkey. The road was no more than pebbles. A mountain stream gurgled. Giant yaks peered at them from rhododendron bushes, then snuffled away uninterested. An occasional bullock cart trundled past.

Dean saw a baby tied into the saddlebag of a horse, like a Seattle kid strapped into a bicycle chair, and as they went ever northward and ever upward, he realized that he was feeling homesick, but not for Seattle. Seattle was lost in time and distance. He realized that such was the human ability to adapt, he was homesick for Kathmandu—and after only two nights in the place.

Because at least Kathmandu was a town. At least Kathmandu was in the Third World. This place was another planet.

Yet again Dean lost all track of time. Maybe they had been traveling for an hour, maybe two, when Chompa pointed to a smudge of white at the head of a glacial valley.

"Home," he said.

It took another hour to reach it, and as they came nearer, Dean made his calculations. It was like a fortress, a vast rectangle on the slopes of a riverbank, the walls maybe a hundred feet high, whitewashed and studded at the top by twenty windows to the south and ten to the east; a flat black-beamed roof; ancient and impregnable.

Dean jumped out and gazed past the monastery to the mountain range. Chompa came up to him and pointed.

"Tibet," he said, then walked onto a bridge.

Then Dean felt a small hand squirm into his, and he looked down at Jesse.

"Dad, I'm scared." A small voice.

And Dean knew what he meant. They were playing well away from home now, heading toward a sort of Bhutanese Alcatraz with the umbilical cords of passports and Amex cards and telephone lines long ago severed.

"Hey, man, I'm scared too," he said. "But what are you gonna tell Mom, huh? She's gonna want to hear the end of the story."

"Yeah."

He felt the boy relax, and they looked across again at the hillside. It seemed to move and shimmer, dotted with long bamboo poles with white cloth fluttering from each one, some fresh and billowing, others tattered, some no more than strings of thread. Lama Norbu came up to them and explained.

"Prayer flags," he said. "The prayers are stitched into the silk and then offered up to the wind."

"But why . . . ?" And the answer came to him as he spoke. "Impermanence, right?"

"Correct."

And Dean felt a small surge of pride.

Hand in hand, father and son crossed the bridge and followed the others along a flagstoned path winding up the hill. Dean dropped to one knee and drew his hand along the stones. They were smooth, flattened by centuries of sandaled feet, and intricately laid without need of mortar.

As they came closer, they heard the familiar mantra from hundreds of voices.

"Om mani padone hum."

And to Dean, it seemed as if they were walking toward a giant beehive. Closer still, and the sound mingled with the slapping of sandaled feet running on flagstones, punctuated by the excited squealing of youthful voices.

The group turned a corner and came to an open gate guarded by two statues: one was of a warrior holding a snarling, straining tiger by a leash, the other a man in robes holding a yak by its reins.

Jesse poked out his tongue at the tiger and whispered to Dean.

"A yak is a Tibetan cow."

"Check," Dean whispered back.

They stopped at the gate. Lama Norbu pushed it open and led them into a courtyard fifty yards square, cloistered on three sides with doors leading away from it. A group of boy monks ran across the courtyard chasing a ball, and men in maroon robes looked down at them from windows and, farther up, from the castellated ramparts.

"Welcome to our home," Lama Norbu said, but his smile could not hide his exhaustion. To Dean, it seemed as if he had made his last effort. He had gone halfway around the world, and now he could relax, and perhaps—Dean remembered Chompa's words in the coffee shop—the relaxation would be terminal.

The children were staring at the game. It seemed to have no rules. The ball was flung from one end of the courtyard to the other. The boys chased it, robes flapping, sandals slapping. The first to reach it kicked it against the wall. It rebounded, and the chase began again.

Jesse dropped Dean's hand and slowly began to walk toward them, with Raju a pace behind and Gita in the rear, and Dean remembered the day he and Lisa went to see Jesse in his new school. They had watched through the fence and had seen a big kid come up and push Jesse. Lisa had started forward, but Dean had pulled her back, just as Jesse hit the kid in the belly and walked on. He was his father's son; he knew how to deal with bullies, and now here he was, half a world away from home, walking toward fifty strangers in robes without so much as a backward glance.

The monks saw them, and the game stopped. For a moment they stared at the newcomers, then ran toward them, smiling and laughing, and surrounded them, and Dean could no longer see the little blond head.

"Some of them are also reincarnations of past lamas," Lama Norbu said. "The name for them is *tulkus*."

Dean nodded; then he saw the group split up, and three of the older boys lead Jesse, Raju, and Gita to a staircase.

"Where are they taking them?" Dean asked.

"To their rooms. Come with me. I want to show you something."

"Yes, but what about . . ." Dean wanted to know the sleeping arrangements. The old man had said "their rooms," which meant splitting him up from Jesse, but the Lama was hurrying away now, and Dean had to trot to catch him.

He stopped at a portico, where three monks were crouched over a table. Dean had never seen such intricacy. The mandala was six feet in diameter, a giant, multicolored jigsaw made of sand, symmetrical, it seemed, to the nearest grain. The oldest monk delicately picked out a pinch of red sand from one of a group of pots, held it between thumb and forefinger, then placed it in the pattern and smoothed it over.

Dean whistled.

"They began making this mandala the day I left," Lama Norbu said. "Now it is almost complete. It represents the natural perfection of the universe."

"Beautiful," Dean said. "But why sand?"

"To show the impermanence of all within the universe. So when it is completed, it is destroyed with a simple gesture." He swept his hand over the mandala. "Like this."

Dean had raised his camera, then lowered it again.

Impermanence—that word again. Perhaps it might be a minor insult to take a snapshot of impermanence; to make a record of impermanence might be something of a contradiction. Maybe the mandala should stay in the memory. Lama Norbu smiled at him, and he felt that he had passed some sort of test.

Then Sangay came up to them and bowed to Dean.

"Come," he said. "I will show you your room."

Dean followed him up a flagstone staircase and out onto a rampart, and Sangay pointed north to Tibet.

A million-dollar view, Dean thought, and idly wondered how his realtor would price this place.

His room was spartan, just a bed and a washstand and a window overlooking the courtyard.

"If it is all right," Sangay said, "Jesse will stay with Raju tonight. Gita, of course, has her own room, but Raju needs a friend. He is nervous."

"That kid?" Dean said. "The circus boy? Nervous?"

"He is all right in the city," Sangay said. "But here . . . this is different."

Dean threw his bag on the bed, and they went back down to the courtyard. The children were playing with the boy monks, and Jesse waved to him. At home already, Dean thought; almost as if he were born in the place.

They crossed to a portico where a group of monks were haranguing one another. Dean stopped to watch. One yelled at his partner and shook his fist. Another leaped in the air and kicked like a ballet dancer. Those being harangued listened in silence, then when their partners had finished, they made their own points, leaping, stamping, slapping hands. Dean glanced at Sangay, his face a question mark.

"It is a philosophical debate," the monk said. "A duel of logic."

To Dean, it looked more like karate.

Sangay pointed and began translating.

"That one says, 'A glass of water is a home for a fish and a drink for a human being. Which one is right?' And that one answers, 'Relatively, they are both right. The water is a home and a drink. There has never been a disagreement between a man and a fish. But ultimately, they are both wrong, because neither water or home exists.'"

Dean blinked. "Who wins?" Which made Sangay squeal with laughter.

"Nobody wins," he said.

And Dean was about to ask what the point was, when a young monk stepped between them.

"But there is a loser," he said to Dean. "The first one who contradicts himself."

"How can you have a loser and not a winner?"

A fair question, Dean thought, but the young monk shook his head and chuckled.

"Very good," he said. "Very Western. You must be a Christian."

"I was born a Christian."

"But you still are," the monk insisted, "if you look for duality in life—the good, the bad; the winner, the loser. In the same way, you Christians believe in God because it makes you sure that you exist. You exist because God created you."

"Maybe," Dean said. "Anyway I'm more Christian than I am a Buddhist."

The monk nodded. "May I make a suggestion?" he said. "Start to think the other way round. God exists because you exist. You created God."

It was the tone as much as the content—patronizing, smart-ass—that made Dean angry.

"What do you know?" he said. "Hiding away in your castle, arguing about fish. What do you understand about life?" He waited. The young monk just smiled. "About passion?" The smile broadened. "What about love?" The monk shrugged. "You Buddhists talk of detachment, of giving up all passions—"

"No, no, mister," the monk said. "You misunderstand Buddhism. You can keep all your passions if you give up your ego."

"What?" The word of bafflement came out like a quack.

"I said you can have the strongest, deepest, most endless emotions—if you are able to give up that *you*."

The monk smiled again and turned away. Dean

slapped his left hand on his biceps and snapped his fingers. There, he said to himself. There's a hand signal for you, an all-American fuck-you signal.

He was about to shout the man back when he saw Chompa come out of a doorway and call to the children. He had three *katas* in his hand, and as they ran to him, he handed one to each child, then led them away.

"The Abbot will see them now," Sangay said.

And maybe it was the patronizing monk who did it, but Dean suddenly became competitive. Go on Jesse, he said to himself. Win.

The Abbot's room was a clutter of paintings, chairs, and tables and overflowed with books. On an altar next to the window stood a large, framed photograph of Lama Dorje. On a table opposite the door, four conical red hats had been placed side by side. They were old, faded, and identical down to the smallest stain. The Abbot sat on a high-backed chair with Lama Norbu standing by his side.

The door opened, and Chompa ushered Raju in, then closed the door behind him. The boy blinked and looked around the room, open-mouthed.

"Come in, Raju," the Abbot said, smiling at him. "Come in, friend of little monkeys."

Shyly he went up to the old man, presented his *kata*, and received it back over his shoulder.

"Now," the Abbot said. "I have a question for you." He pointed to the hats, and Raju glanced at them. "I want you to choose the one you like best."

Raju went across to the table, then turned.

"But they are all the same," he said.

"Yes," the Abbot said. "They are all the same, yet each one is different."

Raju turned again and touched the one on the right. The Abbot placed his hands together and bowed, and said, "Thank you, Raju."

For a moment the boy stood uncertainly gazing at them; then he realized that the two men wanted nothing more from him. He went to the door, opened it, and looked back. Lama Norbu flapped his hands as if shooing geese, and Raju went out, squeezing past Gita as Chompa showed the girl in.

"Welcome, Gita," the Abbot said, "friend of starving tigers."

He made the same request. Gita strode across to the table and chose the hat on the right.

Next to Jesse.

"Welcome, Jesse Long-Ears," the Abbot said. "I have heard a lot about you."

When Jesse heard what was asked of him, he shrugged, looked for a while at the hats, then picked up the same one as the others had chosen and slapped it on his head. It covered his face and rested on his lower lip. Blindly he turned round and said, "This one," in a muffled voice.

"That is Lama Dorje's hat," the Abbot said, trembling as if it were made of china. "So please be careful with it."

Jesse pushed it to the back of his head, winked at them, replaced it, and ran out to find his father.

The room was silent now. The two men looked at each other, then went to the window and looked down into the courtyard. Lama Norbu saw Dean by the mandala. He had his notebook out and was sketching it, but he looked up as Jesse ran toward him and leaped into his arms.

The pain zipped through him again and shuddered down his left arm. He winced and turned to the Abbot.

"I think I have very little time, Your Holiness," he said.

"Then we must ask the old one," the Abbot said. "Although I believe you know the answer already. And in the end only you can decide."

In all the years in the monastery, Lama Norbu had never met the old man. His existence was even doubted by some of the younger monks. His chamber was musty with age and fetid with claustrophobia, the walls hung from floor to ceiling with faded *tankas*. The old man sat on a black throne and wore scarlet robes and a five-pronged metal helmet. At his feet sat an attendant with a notebook, waiting to note his sayings and attempt to translate.

Lama Norbu and a group of older monks squeezed together in front of him, hidden by a veil of silk.

The Lama stared at him and waited. The old man's face was delicate and feminine, without wrinkle or eyelash or eyebrow. His expression was blank, as if asleep. He had been told the tales of the three children and given the charts. Now he closed his eyes, took one deep breath, and entered the transitional world between men and the gods.

Lama Norbu felt his heart batter his rib cage. Claustrophobia was like a pillow on his face.

Suddenly the old man's arms jerked upright, his spine arched in violent convulsion, he slumped forward and began to speak in a high voice that did not seem human.

And the attendant wrote down the sounds, until the spirit that inhabited the old man departed and he slumped to the floor.

Dean was becoming impatient. He had stood on the ramparts for nearly an hour and nothing was happening. It was okay for the monks to wander around down there in the courtyard, all unconcerned; they'd each had a lifetime of meditation, or lifetimes if they were to be believed. They had long attention spans. Dean just wished the old Lama and the Abbot would come to a decision, one way or another.

The three children stood apart. Gita was by the south wall, Raju opposite her, fifty yards across the courtyard, thronged now with monks. Jesse sat against the west wall with Chompa, occasionally looking up at Dean and waving. Each one was preoccupied, Jesse learning how to use a rosary, Gita having her hair braided by Ani-La, Raju playing the Gameboy.

Then, as one, they looked up when a door

opened and Lama Norbu entered the courtyard followed by a group of elderly lamas.

A monk stepped out of the crowd. He was carrying a whip. He walked up to Lama Norbu, bowed, then took his place behind him. The old man stopped in the center of the courtyard looking east; then slowly he began to turn.

Dean held his breath. He had not known how he would react. It seemed a century ago that he had pacified Lisa by saying that it wouldn't be Jesse, that they'd found another candidate, that the odds were stacked against a foreigner. Though he wasn't a betting man, he'd figured that an old Tibetan lama would rather inhabit the body of a Kathmandu kid than a supporter of the Seattle Seahawks . . . but when Lama Norbu walked toward Raju, Dean felt a tug of disappointment. Maybe it was the American in him, but he knew now that, whatever the consequences, he had wanted Jesse to be the Chosen One. Ever since he had accepted the plane tickets from the old man, he had felt that it would pay the monks back many times over if Jesse were the one, because otherwise it was a terrible waste of time and money. But even as he thought this, Dean realized that he was rationalizing, that he wanted Jesse to be chosen because it was un-American just to take part, and it was certainly un-American to come second, Buddhism or no Buddhism.

As the old man prostrated himself in front of Raju, Dean looked at his son and saw the disappointment on his face, then he looked at Gita playing with her plait and feigning boredom.

"O my teacher," Lama Norbu said to Raju, "I am so happy to have found you again."

His voice echoed around the courtyard, and the monk cracked his whip.

That's it then, Dean thought. Time, as the cowboys said, to piss on the fire and call in the dogs, 'cos the hunt's over. He was about to turn away and head for the stairs when he saw the old man make his way toward Gita. Dean watched, thinking that he was going to offer his condolences, but again the old man prostrated himself. Again he said the same words. Again the monk cracked the whip.

Dean was stunned. He didn't get it. How could there be two? How could Lama Dorje separate his soul, like some kind of spiritual amoeba? Now it was a double insult to Jesse.

He ran across the parapet and down the stairs and reached the courtyard just in time to see Lama Norbu prostrate himself yet again, this time in front of Jesse, and through the crowd of excited monks, he saw Jesse mimic him, go down on his knees, the boy and the old man touching foreheads. Then the old man's voice boomed a third time:

"O my teacher, I am so happy to have found you at last."

The whip cracked again. Slowly and painfully but with a broad smile, Lama Norbu got to his feet and beckoned Raju and Gita to come over.

Dean joined the circle of monks crowding around them as the old man beamed at the three children.

"I am truly happy," he said. "Three times happy."

And it was Jesse who put the question, Jesse who had never been backward at coming forward.

"But how can we all be Lama Dorje?"

That's my boy, Dean said to himself. How indeed?

"It is very rare," the old man said, "but it has happened before. Separate manifestations of the body, the speech, and the mind. None of these three exist without the others. All of us are attached, like the world to the universe. But remember this"—he looked from one to the other, then to Dean—"the most important thing of all is to feel compassion for all beings, to give of oneself, and above all to pass on knowledge like the Buddha did. After his Enlightenment, Buddha devoted the rest of his years to helping others. And he is still helping us. Even now."

The speech had exhausted him and he leaned against one of the monks for support. Then Jesse saw his father, ran to him, and leaped into his arms.

"Dad, Dad," he burbled enthusiastically, "we are all Lama Dorje. Raju, Gita, and me."

"I know. Big day, Jesse Long-Ears."

It was the first time that he had used the nickname the old man had given his son, and Jesse grinned at him. The demon of jealousy had been defeated.

"Which one are you?" he said. "The body, speech, or mind?"

"The body," he said. "No, the mind." He shrugged. "I don't know. It doesn't matter." He squirmed out of Dean's grip and slithered to the ground. "I gotta go, Dad. The Abbot wants to see us."

As he ran off, Dean thought to himself: I just got myself one third of a *tulku*.

The courtyard emptied fast, and Dean saw Lama Norbu make his way toward a door, then stumble, clutch his chest, and lean heavily against the wall. He ran to him and looked into the tired face.

"Hey," he said. "You okay?"

"Yes, thank you." The words were a wheeze. "A little overcome, that's all."

"Well, it's been a pretty emotional time for all of us."

The old man took a deep breath and attempted a smile. "I'm afraid I'm not a very good example of Buddhist detachment." And the smile became a chuckle. "Children," he said. "We are all children."

Slowly he took off his wristwatch and from the folds of his robes took out the cracked wooden bowl that the wild hermit had given him.

"This is for Jesse," he said, then placed the watch into it. "And this is for you. My work is done. Now I can rest."

He handed the bowl to Dean and chuckled again. "I can even go back to Tibet," he said, then pushed himself away from the wall and wagged a finger in Dean's face. "You still don't believe in reincarnation, do you?"

Dean shrugged, and the old man wheezed away, laughing at some private joke, and climbed the three steps to the chapel door, and his laughter became a hacking cough.

Dean gave him a moment to settle himself, then looked in. The place was in darkness, and it took him a while for his eyes to adjust. Then he saw Lama Norbu settle himself on a cushion, take off his shoes, and assume the lotus position. It was a small room, unfurnished except for a prayer wheel at the door and an altar. It was windowless, airless, claustrophobic. The Lama did not see him. His eyes were closed in meditation. Behind him an old monk sat at a sewing machine; the only noise was his foot on the treadle, accompanied by the heavy breathing of the Lama, and now Dean felt that he was intruding and silently turned away.

Nine

At first, as he struggled awake, Dean thought that the noise was the bellowing of a hundred bulls, but no bull could have sounded so mournful. He blinked, unsure for a moment, where he was; then he padded out of bed to the window and opened the shutters. Two men stood on the tiled roof opposite. They were dressed in robes and turbans, and blew on eight-foot horns, whose bells were resting on the tiles.

It was the most grievous sound he had ever heard. He turned, dressed quickly, and ran out and down the stairs to the courtyard, while Chompa's voice looped through his brain like a mantra, "Not completely well, but very strong."

And suddenly it was important to see the old

man again, even if, to judge from the sound of the horns, it was too late.

The door of the chapel was closed. It creaked as he pushed it open. Lama Norbu was in the same position as he had left him. The old monk still sat by the sewing machine; the sound of the Lama's breathing was more labored now.

Dean went in, nodded a greeting at the monk, and sat opposite the Lama, his back against the wall, and began his vigil.

Now that he was a *tulku*, Jesse was no longer afraid, no longer homesick or apprehensive about the boys in their robes. Everyone seemed to want to make him happy; grown men bowed before him, and he began to feel important and wondered if such a feeling were a sin.

The preparation had taken hours. He had been bathed and scented with oils. He had been dressed in a maroon and yellow robe and a yellow hat like a parrot's beak. Then the two monks led him out into the courtyard, and he saw Gita and Raju waiting for him; they were dressed identically—spirit, mind, and body. Gita smiled at him, and her plaited hair swung. Raju looked solemn.

Then they were led, side by side, across the courtyard to the prayer room. As they came in, Jesse gazed around him, at the high, vaulted ceiling, at the colorful *tankas* on the walls, the altar, and the gold Buddha.

Monks sat cross-legged looking at them, while others gazed down from balconies. Everything was maroon. Every face smiled. He felt like Siddhartha leaving the palace to see the world, and he half expected to be showered with rose petals and lotus blossoms.

Then the cacophony began. Drums began to beat, trumpets blared, tambourines and percussion instruments shrieked and clattered, and each monk, as he passed, prostrated himself.

At the far end of the room, in front of a large throne and an altar, three small thrones, of beautifully carved wood inlaid with gold leaf, were placed side by side.

Jesse was shown to the one on the left, Raju on the right, and Gita took her seat in the middle, smiling at each of them as if she owned the place.

Then Jesse settled back. He felt like the President of the United States, and as the first monk came forward with an offering of a bracelet, Jesse's only worry was that the kids at school weren't going to believe any of this.

A clattering noise brought Dean groggily awake out of a nightmare. He looked up to see a monk in the doorway. It was the man he had argued with. He had bumped into the prayer wheel. The man nodded to him and came across to sit next to him, and only then did Dean see the others. Three men were standing around Lama Norbu, one touching his wrist, another feeling for a pulse in his neck.

"Yesterday," Dean whispered, "he was talking about going back to Tibet."

The monk nodded.

"How long can he sit like that?" Dean asked. "He hasn't moved since last night."

"He has controlled all his emotion and attachment," the monk said, "so he can sit like a mountain, serene and unmovable for days, and meditate like the ocean, deep and vast, for as long as he likes. And when he wants to depart from this body, he can do so, with his choice."

"You mean, he can choose when he goes?" Dean could not believe what the man was saying and thought that perhaps he might have misunderstood.

"Yes, he has choice because he has no attachment. When you have attachment, then the attachment takes over and you become no choice."

Dean continued to stare at the old man.

"What happens when he dies?"

"He will stop his breathing and the beating of his heart, but he will remain in meditation because the mind cannot die. You know, life and death is like changing clothes; before you wear the new one and after you changed the old one, you have to be naked for at least one second. This is the transitional state known as *bardo*."

"But why is he choosing to go now?"

The monk shrugged again. "Why not?" he said. "Maybe it is the greatest lesson because only the separation makes you value the togetherness. And also like the Buddha. He passed away because it teaches us the impermanence."

Dean did not understand. Maybe he never would, but still he tried.

"Doesn't it make you sad?" he asked,

"I will miss him," the monk said, "but I am not sad. Because I try to think that the life and death is like a dream, and then I try to awake within the awakening." He smiled. "You know, Lama Norbu used to say that when we go to sleep, we should think that we are awaking, and then, when we are awaking in the morning, we should think that we are beginning to sleep and dream. And I also know that he will come back. Not because of the karma, not because of the force of some other conditions, but by the power of his own compassion, to help other beings as a bodhisattva."

And Dean wished that he had the faith. He wished that he could believe.

In the prayer room the ceremony was coming to an end. The Abbot took off the children's hats, slowly poured a drop of water on each scalp, and cut a lock of hair. Then he stepped back and bowed once as the monks began to file past the thrones, each one with an offering of beads, jewelry, and trinkets.

Jesse watched the treasure piling up in front of him and accepted the obeisances with a nod and a smile, then turned as he saw a monk come in, go to the Abbot, and whisper something. The Abbot nodded, held up his hand, and began to chant, and as he spoke, the others joined in with a low murmur. Jesse glanced at Gita and saw that she was crying and that Raju was knuckling his eyes, and instinctively he knew that Lama Norbu had gone.

He looked up above the altar and for a moment

he thought he saw the old man; then Jesse closed his eyes and heard the Lama's voice as if the old man were sitting next to him.

"Jesse, Raju, Gita," the Lama said.

"They are chanting the Heart Sutra," he said. "It is a beautiful prayer. Learn it. Keep it with you in your hearts, always. It will help you."

The children closed their eyes as the monks chanted, and Lama Norbu, in the state of *bardo*, chanted with them:

> "O Shariputra, form is empty,
>   Emptiness is form.
>   Form is none other than emptiness,
>   Emptiness is none other than form."

Jesse's lips moved silently as he followed the old man's words, and he forced his eyes tightly shut to hold back the tears.

> "O Shariputra, all that exist
>   Are expressions of Emptiness;
>   Not born, not destroyed, not stained, not pure,
>   Without loss, without gain.
>   So in emptiness there is no form,
>   No sensation, conception, discrimination,
>   awareness.
>   No eye, ear, nose, tongue, body, mind.
>   No color, sound, smell, taste, touch, existing
>   thing . . ."

And halfway round the world, in the Dharma Center in Seattle, Kempo Tenzin spoke on the phone, and Lisa listened.

"No realm of sight, no realm of consciousness.
No ignorance and no end to ignorance,
No old age and death.
No suffering, no cause of or end to suffering.
No path, no wisdom, and no gain.
No gain, thus bodhisattvas live
In perfect understanding with no hindrance,
Of mind, no hindrance, therefore no fear.
Far beyond deluded thoughts,
This is Nirvana."

Jesse opened his eyes. The place was still now, the monks silent and at prayer, and his father was kneeling in front of him.

"Dad," he whispered, "Lama Norbu just said, 'No eye, no ear, no nose . . .'"

He pointed to himself. "No Jesse, no Lama . . ."

He pointed at his father, "No you, no death, no fear."

And he smiled even as the tears began to drip down his cheeks and stain his robe.

Dean wiped them away and helped him off his stool, and they walked out of the prayer room, with Gita and Ani-La behind, then Raju and Sangay, with Chompa at the rear.

Slowly they crossed the courtyard to the chapel. The shutters had been pulled open, and they climbed the steps and looked inside.

Lama Norbu sat as he had sat for a night and a morning, a *kata* covering his face.

Well, old man, Dean thought, the cup is broken, but where is the tea?

Jesse bowed a farewell, then took Dean's hand, turned, and led him to the portico, where the Abbot and a group of monks were standing beside the mandala. It was finished now. The Abbot waited until the children and their chaperons had taken a last look at it, then, with one sweep of his arm, scattered the sand to the wind.

Epilogue

There had been a surprise at the airport—a slash of maroon standing beside Lisa in the Arrivals Hall and smiling chubbily. The reunion had been a flurry of hugs and kisses, and Lisa mopping back tears. She'd said that she and Kempo Tenzin had become friendly over the past two weeks, that he had helped her whenever she had been lonely or worried, but Dean did not hear any of this, because during the hugging and the kissing she'd told him that she was pregnant.

She had worked it out; it must have been the night of Lama Norbu's visit, a sort of blessing, an example of cause and effect. It was a continuation.

Now she and Jesse sat on a pier at the marina,

watching for Dean. Lisa had a wooden casket on her lap. She fiddled with it, tried it this way and that, then gave up. There was a secret hinge. Jesse opened it. There were two drawers. Jesse pulled out the top one and took out a white scarf.

"This is Lama Norbu's *kata*," he said.

Then he pulled out the lower drawer. It was filled with ashes.

"And this is Lama Norbu."

Lisa nodded. Last night, in her practical way, she had asked about Customs, asked if the U.S.A. accepted the remains of a Tibetan lama, and Jesse had said no problem because the Customs guy was a Buddhist.

Then they saw Dean coming round the bay in the *Mary Jane*, the little twenty-foot chugger that might have to be sold if things didn't improve; but the idea didn't seem to bother Dean all that much. The problems were the same, but his attitude had changed. Dean was going to be okay.

As the little boat bumped the quay, Jesse did a cartwheel.

"Mom, Dad, I'm Raju," he said.

"And what about Gita?" Lisa said.

Jesse posed like a ballerina and imitated the girl's voice. "Oh Gita, the secret society of King Cobra."

Then giggling, he jumped aboard and helped Lisa into the bow. Dean pushed off, and they chugged out into the bay. It was a dull day with a heavy swell, and it took twenty minutes to get far enough out so that, when they turned, they had a perfect view of the Seattle skyline and the mountains.

Dean cut the engine, picked up the old bowl from beneath his seat, and watched as Jesse filled it with the ashes. Then he looked at the old man's watch—it was almost time. In Nepal, Gita would be ready to scatter ashes under the big tree, and in Bhutan, Raju, who had stayed on to become a boy monk, would be placing the remains in a *kata* tied to balloons, preparing to send Lama Norbu skyward.

A moment passed, and Jesse said, "It's time," without needing to ask. He leaned over the side with the bowl in both hands and placed it gently in the water.

Dean looked at his son. He was sure that he would carry out Lama Norbu's wishes one way or another, to spread the Dharma in the West. If Buddhism were not exactly in his blood, it was in his soul, and he had a responsibility to the others, for what were mind and speech without body, or body and speech without mind, or mind and body without speech?

He had much to ask the boy, many unanswered questions; he would ask Jesse when he grew up.

As he stared at the bobbing bowl, it seemed in Dean's imagination to be moving against the current.

And Jesse smiled.

Production Notes

Against the backdrop of the Himalayas, on the roof of the world, filming began on Bernardo Bertolucci's long-awaited epic, *Little Buddha*, in September 1992.

It was the climax of years of planning and preparation by Bertolucci, Producer Jeremy Thomas, and the production team—including cinematographer Vittorio Storaro and Production and Costume Designer James Acheson—and was the team's first return to the East since their triumph with *The Last Emperor,* which collected nine Academy Awards including Best Director and Best Picture. The screenplay is by Mark Peploe and Rudy Wurlitzer from a story by Bertolucci.

In addition to his exceptional production team,

Bertolucci has assembled an international cast headed by Keanu Reeves as Prince Siddhartha, with Chris Isaak, Bridget Fonda, and newcomer Alex Wiesendanger in the modern roles. Ying Ruocheng, memorably seen in *The Last Emperor,* also stars.

The film is a CiBy 2000/Recorded Picture Company coproduction.

The breathtaking, and sometimes near-impossible, locations for *Little Buddha* included the Kathmandu Valley, the Terai lowlands of Nepal, and the remote mountain kingdom of Bhutan, land of the Thunder Dragon. The modern American setting was Seattle, where filming was concluded in February 1993.

The extensively researched project received the blessing of his holiness the Dalai Lama at a meeting with Bertolucci and Jeremy Thomas in 1991 and one of Tibetan Buddhism's most senior lamas, Dzongsar Khyenste Rinpoche, acted as technical advisor to the production.

One of the most ambitious production ventures of recent times, the film employed an army of artists and craftsmen to recreate the exotic pre-Christian world of Prince Siddhartha's court and the vitality and color of modern-day Kathmandu and Bhutan. Many of the locations used were legendary historical sites such as the holy *stupa* of Bodnath in Kathmandu, and the spectacular ancient royal palace complexes of Patan and Bhaktapur and the massive fortified monastary of Paro Dzong in Bhutan.

Recreating their impressive record of filming in

hitherto inaccessible locations—as with the Forbidden City in Beijing for *The Last Emperor*—Bertolucci and Thomas obtained permission to film in the Kingdom of Bhutan, which only admits 2000 tourists a year, and even more significantly were allowed to film inside the monastery of Paro Dzong. No film crew has ever before been given access to this Buddhist mountain stronghold.

The History of the Project

In the early part of 1991, producer Jeremy Thomas and director Bernardo Bertolucci began planning their third project together. As ever, they had several films in mind. But the theme of reincarnation—a challenge to modern Western values—was one they could not set aside. At the same time, Francis Bouygues, the French entrepreneur who had created one of the largest construction companies in the world, was in the process of launching CiBy 2000, a film financing company committed to supporting the greatest creative talents of world cinema. Bouygues, Thomas, and Bertolucci agreed on a deal for the development and production of the new film, now titled *Little Buddha*.

Bertolucci was first introduced to Buddhism at

the age of 21 when the Italian writer Elsa Morante gave him a book on the life of Milarepa, one of the great Tibetan Buddhist saints. During the 1980s Bertolucci became increasingly drawn toward distant cultures, landscapes, and faces in what he smilingly calls "an invincible attraction to become an orientalist." Shortly after the Academy Award triumph of *The Last Emperor*, he was approached about filming a biography of the Buddha and, although this project was not to be, the Milarepa book came back to mind. After rereading the story Bertolucci was to become increasingly interested in Tibetan Buddhism and stories of recognitions of reincarnated lamas. During 1989–90 he began to investigate this phenomenon and started studying Buddhism by reading the old books of Sutras and the great poem *Buddhacarita*, by Ashvaghosha. With the help of different Tibetan lamas Bertolucci began to enter a world he had only vaguely known before.

Bertolucci was particularly fascinated by the idea of a relationship between an old lama and a child whom he believes to be the reincarnation of his teacher. "What is so special in this relationship is the fact that the old lama has two different attitudes toward the child. One is a normal paternal or grandfatherly affection. The other is respect toward the child who is the reincarnation of his teacher. I think that mixture of affection and respect is exactly the attitude we should have with all children. I found this relationship, which happens every time a lama finds a *tulku,* very poetic and vibrant."

By the end of 1991 Bertolucci had written a fifty page story that was developed into a screenplay with Rudy Wurlitzer and Mark Peploe. In 1991, Bertolucci and Jeremy Thomas traveled to Vienna to meet with His Holiness the Dalai Lama, who gave his blessing to the project.

On September 20, 1992, in the courtyard of the majestic Chokyi Nyima Monastery in Bodnath, the cast and crew of *Little Buddha* assembled for their first day's shooting.

The crew numbered 120 from Europe, 100 locally hired Nepalis and Indians, and hundreds of subcontracted local people. The cosmopolitan nature of the production was continuously demonstrated during the preparation of this film, on a scale never before seen in Nepal or Bhutan. It was the fruition of a dream which began many years ago, and which the production team had been planning for many months.

About Buddhism

Little Buddha takes its inspiration from the belief in reincarnation, which is fundamental to Buddhism. Unlike younger religions, such as Christianity and Islam, Buddhism professes no belief in an original creator. It does not proclaim itself as a religion in the ordinary sense, nor does it practice evangelism. Instead it proposes an endless and spiraling continuum of being, in which good and bad acts— karma—affect the upward or downward progress of individual reincarnations, and the interdependency of all sentient beings.

Buddhism is better described as a world view—a quest for spiritual truth. It relies on the practitioner experiencing its teachings rather than simply learning them, a quest for self-knowledge rather than a belief system. Buddhism is a nondogmatic tradition, not founded on a book or articles of faith but stemming from a respect for the manner in which the Buddha conducted his own search for spiritual truth and from which an array of spiritual practices, ranging from moral precepts to meditative practices, has developed.

The Buddha lived approximately two thousand five hundred years ago. He rejected the caste system and some of the mystical aspects of the Hindu religion of the time he was born into. However, his teachings share the Hindu doctrines of reincarnation and karma, along with many yogic practices. In common with Hindus, Buddhists strive for release from the cycle of rebirth—but where the Hindu ideal is to be reunited with the creator, the Buddhist ideal is to reach Nirvana, the state of perfect and final peace reached upon enlightenment.

Enlightenment is attained by mastering the Four Noble Truths:

Suffering exists.
Suffering has an identifiable cause—desire.
The taming of desire can end suffering.
Desire can be tamed by following the
    Eightfold Path.

The Eightfold Path is:
Right Understanding
Right Thought
Right Speech
Right Action

Right Livelihood
Right Effort
Right Mindfulness
Right Concentration.

This essentially subdivides into the three elements of Wisdom, Ethics and Meditation. There is no hierarchy to the Eightfold Path: all the elements have to be developed together.

The path which the Buddha found and called The Middle Way neither embraces nor denounces the world but strives for nonattachment. Once the illusion of self has been cast off, enlightenment can be achieved.

Buddhism was spread by translation and example, becoming the principal spiritual force for the many diverse cultures of the East. It spread to the countries we now know as India, Nepal, Tibet, Sri Lanka, Myanmar, Thailand, Vietnam, Korea, China, Japan, Cambodia, and Mongolia. As Buddhism grew and spread, different teachings and practices began to evolve: for example, Tantric Buddhism and Zen Buddhism. However the complexities of the diverse forms of Buddhism which now exist do not detract from the simplicity of the core ideas, which remain universal for Buddhist practitioners throughout the world.

Reincarnation is a concept central to all forms of Buddhism, however reincarnation in the form depicted in the film *Little Buddha* is not universal within the Buddhist world. The reincarnation of an individual lama into a specific other person or persons, who then has to be found—the concept of *Rinpoches* and *tulkus*—is specific to Tibetan Buddhism. The Buddhist culture and rituals shown in the film *Little Buddha* are also of Tibetan Buddhist origins.

The Life of Prince Siddhartha — Historical Background

The date of birth of the man who was to become known as the Buddha is not known, but is estimated to be approximately two thousand five hundred years ago. What is generally agreed is that he was born in Lumbini, situated in the Terai region of what is now known as the Kingdom of Nepal. He was given the name Siddhartha and took the clan name Gautama. He was the son of a King or leader of the Sakya clan, Suddhodana, who ruled the Terai from its capital Kapilvista. His mother, Maya, died a week after giving birth and her place was taken by her sister Prajapati.

It is said that the birth of this great-man-to-be was heralded by a prophetic dream that he entered his mother's womb in the form of an elephant, she carried him for ten months, and gave birth to him standing up. As soon as Siddhartha was born he stood and walked.

Not long after the birth of Prince Siddhartha, a sage and astrologer named Asita came to Kapilvista and prophesied that Siddhartha would grow up to be a fully enlightened buddha, a teacher of men. Far from being happy to hear this, Suddhodana decided to shut his son off from the world. As the young boy grew up it became increasingly difficult to chaperone him at all times so three magnificent palaces were built for him, one for the hot season, one for the cool season, and one for the rainy season. Siddhartha was confined to these palaces where he grew up into a kind and handsome young man who excelled at sport. At the age of sixteen Siddhartha won the hand of his beautiful cousin Yasodhara by beating his many rival suitors in a series of contests. Yasodhara would bear him a son— Rahula.

Despite the stringent security, news of the outside world reached Siddhartha and made him curious and restless. Trips to the outside were arranged and it was on these trips, always accompanied by his groom, Channa, that Siddhartha encountered old age, sickness, and death. This had a profound effect on him. He was compelled to understand the nature of suffering and to find a solution to it. On one such trip Siddhartha encountered a Sadhu (a wandering holy man) dressed in rags and possessing nothing. A deep conflict arose in his heart. He knew he would have to leave his palace but to do so would mean giving up all his material comforts and, more importantly, leaving his wife and abandoning his duty to his father.

The conflict eventually reached its inevitable climax and, as legend has it, on the night Yasodhara gave birth to Rahula, Siddhartha woke Channa, saddled up his horse, Kantaka, and the two of then fled the palace in the dead of the night. Prince Siddhartha was twenty-nine years old. They rode toward the River Anoma, on the boundary of the Sakya kingdom. Siddhartha hacked off his hair and exchanged his fine clothes with those of a wandering holy man and instructed Channa to return to Kapilvista. Thus began Siddhartha's great spiritual quest.

Siddhartha sought out the distinguished teachers of the day, and became a proficient student of exalted spiritual states, but he remained unsatisfied. He went to the jungle near Uruvela and submitted himself to the most grueling form of asceticism in the belief that mortifying the body and subjecting it to the most extreme forms of suffering would overcome suffering itself.

There he burned in the sun, froze at night, and starved himself. He was joined by five Ascetics and they remained together for five years. Siddhartha eventually realized that self-denial brought him no closer to the truth than self-indulgence: to continue would mean dying before finding the solution he was seeking. When he took a little food the five Ascetics left him in disgust. Siddhartha had renounced everything and the only thing left for him to try was a middle way. At a place in India, now known as Bodgaya, Siddhartha sat in meditation under a Bodhi Tree (of the species *ficus religiosa*).

There, as the legend continues, Mara the Tempter, whose role it was to maintain delusion and desire, attempted to undo Siddhartha. When Mara's five beautiful daughters failed to seduce him, his demonic hordes launched an all-out attack. But even his hideous army could not shake Siddhartha from his attempt to attain enlightenment.

Less mythological accounts of this story tell us that after forty-nine days of meditation Siddhartha entered a state of meditative concentration which enabled him to gain the knowledge and insight to remember many former existences, gain knowledge of the workings of karma and how to destroy the imperfections of sensual desire, desire for existence and ignorance. Siddhartha had abandoned the illusion of "I" and understood the true nature of all things. He was no longer Gautama Siddhartha but had become the Awakened One—the Buddha.

It is thought that the Buddha remained under the Bodhi Tree until the great god Brahma Sahampati appealed to him to teach others. He began with the five Ascetics who had rejected him earlier. His spiritual radiance won them over and they began to listen to his teachings of the Four

Noble Truths and the Middle Way. One of the Ascetics, Kordanna, understood at once and became the first Buddhist monk to be ordained and so the Buddha began "to turn the wheel of the dharma," and the community of Buddhist monks began.

The Buddha is believed to have been about thirty-five when he became enlightened. For forty-five years he traveled throughout central-northern India teaching. He is said to have returned to Kapilvista to establish his family on the Path. He died at the age of eighty in Kasia, about one hundred kilometers southeast of Lumbini.

Biographies—
The Filmmakers

DIRECTOR—BERNARDO BERTOLUCCI

Bernardo Bertolucci was born in Parma, Italy, in 1941. Through his father Atillo Bertolucci, a well-known poet, he met the director Pier Paolo Pasolini, and in 1961 he abandoned his studies to work as an assistant director on Pasolini's first film, *Accatone*. The following year he wrote the screenplay of the film which was to be his directorial debut, *La Commare Secca* (The Grim Reaper). The film was acclaimed at the Venice Film Festival and he went on to make his second feature, *Before the Revolution*.

In 1967 Bertolucci was asked by Sergio Leone to write the storyline for *Once Upon a Time in the West*, and soon after he completed his next film as director, *Partner*. In 1969 he directed *The Spider's Stratagem*, and *The Conformist*, his brilliant adaptation of the Alberto Moravia novel, which earned him his reputation as a major figure in contemporary cinema. His reputation was confirmed in 1973 with the enormous critical and commercial success of *Last Tango in Paris*. In 1976 he directed *1900*, the first of several epic historical films. He produced and directed *La Luna* in 1979 and *Tragedy of a Ridiculous Man* in 1981. In 1986 Bertolucci turned to the East and the story of Pu Yi, China's last absolute ruler, in *The Last Emperor*. Bertolucci not only won the Best Director Award at the 1988 Oscars but the film itself gathered a further eight Oscars including Best Picture, and went on to collect numerous awards around the world. After the epic scale of *The Last Emperor* Bertolucci chose to return to a more intimate story, though still working on a large visual canvas, with his 1990 adaptation of the Paul Bowles novel *The Sheltering Sky*, set in the Sahara Desert.

In September 1992 Bertolucci returned to the East to commence shooting *Little Buddha*, which marks his third successive collaboration with Producer Jeremy Thomas and an association of over twenty-five years with Cinematographer Vittorio Storaro.

BERNARDO BERTOLUCCI
FILMOGRAPHY

1990	*The Sheltering Sky*
1987	*The Last Emperor*
1981	*Tragedy of a Ridiculous Man*
1979	*La Luna*
1976	*1900*
1972	*Last Tango in Paris*
1971	*La Salute e Malata* (or *I Poveri Muoiono Prima*) (Doc.)
1969	*The Conformist*
1970	*The Spider's Stratagem*
1968	*Partner*
1967	*Agonia* (Episode of *Love and Hatred*)
1966	*La Via Del Petrolio* (Documentary TV)
	Il Canale (Short documentary)
1964	*Before the Revolution*
1962	*The Grim Reaper*

PRODUCER—JEREMY THOMAS

Cinema has always been a part of Jeremy Thomas's life. He was born in Ealing, London, into a filmmaking family. His childhood ambition was to work in cinema. As soon as he left school he went to work in the cutting rooms, rising through the ranks to become a film editor.

After editing Philippe Mora's *Brother Can You Spare a Dime?* he produced his first film, *Mad Dog*

Morgan in 1974 in Australia. He then returned to England to produce Jerzy Skolimowski's *The Shout*, which won the Grand Prix de Jury at the Cannes Film Festival.

Thomas's films are very individual and his refusal to run with the pack has paid off both artistically and financially. His extensive output includes three films directed by Nicolas Roeg: *Bad Timing, Eureka,* and *Insignificance;* Julien Temple's *The Great Rock and Roll Swindle;* Nagisa Oshima's *Merry Christmas, Mr. Lawrence*; and *The Hit* directed by Stephen Frears.

In 1986 he produced Bernardo Bertolucci's 25-million-dollar epic, *The Last Emperor,* an independently-financed project which was three years in the making. A commercial and critical triumph, the film swept the board at the 1988 Academy Awards, garnering an outstanding nine Oscars, including Best Picture.

Since *The Last Emperor,* Thomas has completed Karel Reisz's *Everybody Wins*; Bertolucci's *The Sheltering Sky*; and David Cronenberg's *Naked Lunch*. In August 1992 he was appointed Chairman of the British Film Institute.

JEREMY THOMAS FILMOGRAPHY

1992   *Naked Lunch*
           Director David Cronenberg
1991   *Everybody Wins*
           Director Karel Reisz

1990	*The Sheltering Sky*
	Director Bernardo Bertolucci
1987	*The Last Emperor*
	Director Bernardo Bertolucci
1985	*Insignificance*
	Director Nicolas Roeg
1983	*The Hit*
	Director Stephen Frears
1982	*Merry Christmas, Mr. Lawrence*
	Director Nagisa Oshima
1979	*Bad Timing*
	Director Nicolas Roeg
1978	*The Great Rock and Roll Swindle*
	Director Julien Temple
1977	*The Shout*
	Director Jerzy Skolimowski
1976	*Mad Dog Morgan*
	Director Philipe Mora

CINEMATOGRAPHER—VITTORIO STORARO

Vittorio Storaro was born in Rome in 1940. He was encouraged by his father to develop an interest in photography and attended the Duca D'Aosta photography school from an early age. He subsequently studied at the Centro Sperimentale di Cinematografia. After spending a period as an apprentice at a photographic studio he became assistant to photographers Aldo Scarvada and Marco Scarpelli.

Storaro has known Bertolucci since 1964 when he worked as a camera assistant on the director's second film, *Before the Revolution*. Thus began a creative partnership that has endured for more than a quarter of a century and a further seven films: *The Conformist; Last Tango in Paris; 1900; La Luna; The Last Emperor; The Sheltering Sky;* and *Little Buddha*.

In 1979 Francis Coppola's *Apocalypse Now* brought Storaro his first Academy Award for Best Photography. Two other Academy Awards followed, in 1981 for Warren Beatty's *Reds*, and in 1988 for Bertolucci's *The Last Emperor*. Other film credits include Coppola's segment of *New York Stories; One From the Heart; Tucker;* and Warren Beatty's *Dick Tracy*. For the past two and a half years Storaro has worked on *Imago Urbis*, a fifteen-part series on Roman Culture of which 11 episodes are finished and the remaining 4 will be shot on completion of *Little Buddha*. Before embarking on this long-term project Storaro ensured that he would be available to work with Bertolucci on *Little Buddha*.

For Storaro cinema is a language of images. "In order to really do my job, I have to use all the elements that are in my hands, like light and shadows, and what Leonardo (da Vinci) called their children—colors—to tell the stories. That's why I think of myself as a writer with light rather than a painter." He sees a clear division in his collaboration with Bertolucci. "He thinks about space and I think about light. So the camera is his pen and light is my pen. Very clear. He doesn't interfere in my field and I don't interfere in his. But we have to listen to each other, absolutely."

The story of *Little Buddha* is divided into four parts—Modern Seattle, Kathmandu, Bhutan, and Ancient India. Each of the locations have their own special atmosphere and light. To emphasize the difference between them and maximize the psychological impact of moving between time frames, Storaro used a combination of 35mm, cinemascope, Vista Vision, and 65mm.

Storaro describes *Little Buddha* as an important human experience. "Any movie is part of our life, some more than others, and there is no doubt that everything I have done up to now was with me on *Little Buddha*. My preproduction for *Little Buddha* was fifty-three years."

Glossary of Names, Titles and Terms Used

BUDDHA: General term for a series of teachers. Usage is distinct from "the Buddha" which refers solely to Gautama Siddhartha.

DHARMA: Range of meanings. At its most general, dharma refers to "universal law." More specifically it relates to one's duty to family, religion, and community.

DURBAR: Royal court, Palace.

DZONG: Fortress and monastery.

GOMPA: Buddhist monastery.

KARMA: The soul's accumulated merit determining its next rebirth.

KATA: White scarf given to lamas.

LAMA: Important religious teacher, not necessarily a monk.

MANDALA: A mystical diagram and meditation tool. In Tantric Buddhism it is a model of both the cosmos and the total human being.

NIRVANA: Enlightenment and release from the cycle of rebirth.

PUJA: Act of worship.

RINPOCHE: "Precious One." Title of honor given to a high lama. Used as a suffix to the name.

SAMSARA: Eternal transmigration of the soul.

STUPA: A large Buddhist monument, usually said to contain holy relics.

SUTRA: Basic Buddhist doctrines.

THANKA: Buddhist scroll painting.

TULKU: Reincarnation of a figure of some distinction.